THE THIN HOUSE

JAKE NICKENS

To Sara Rizzo

[signature]

ISBN-13: 978-0-578-64154-6

This book is dedicated to grandparents—and to the stories they tell their grandchildren.

TABLE OF CONTENTS

PROLOGUE

From the Desk of Agent Seven
Emergency Audit Report #2,176

Upon receiving an emergency alert at 3:37 p.m. Central Standard Time, I departed immediately for Entry Point No. 06—colloquial designation, "The Thin House." Containment efforts were already underway upon my arrival, and minimal direct action was required to subdue the Entity. Property managers Eleanor and Ezekiel Blacklock informed me that, prior to my arrival, a human salesman named James Farsons gained unauthorized access to the property and was lured into the containment zone. This illicit contact led to seven minutes of unrestricted movement by the Entity.

The Entity's escape was largely confined to the basement. I can confirm that neither the main structure nor the protective outer zone was breached. A survey revealed that none of the boarders were seriously harmed during the incident. The salesman in question was fully absorbed into the Entity, and any efforts regarding separation will require executive authorization. The property manager's daughter was traumatized by the experience to some degree, but she received no physical injuries.

This incident marks the first security breach in the 102 years of the Thin House's existence. As per the stipulations outlined in the Blacklocks' employment contract, they were formally warned and reprimanded. Any future rule violations or lapses in security will be considered a breach of contract and grounds for termination. In addition to standard observation and reporting procedures, I recommend an additional, invasive audit in thirty years. The results of said audit should be considered in determining future authorization of Thin House activities.

These remarks constitute my full report. I am available for questioning regarding any points of clarification.

Agent Seven
June 9, 1963

CHAPTER ONE:
THE HOUSE

Finn Anglin's mother parked her car on the side of the road near a small, stone bridge. She stared silently at the bridge, which marked the entrance to her parents' remote property, and she would not get out the car.

"You can walk from here," she insisted. "Get your bags."

His otherwise polite, considerate, and responsible mother seemed oddly uncomfortable, and Finn couldn't believe she expected him to walk the rest of the way alone in the Louisiana heat.

"I can't see the house from here. Is it far?" Finn asked.

"No, honey. Just cross the bridge and follow the dirt road. You'll see it once you clear that hill. I'm sure your grandparents will be watching for you."

"You're sure you don't want to say hi? We're already here."

Finn's mother didn't say anything. She only shook her head softly and looked away. Finn didn't push the subject; it was unpleasant but familiar territory. In eleven years, Finn had never met his grandparents, and his mother had only spoken about them a handful of times. Finn always paid attention when she mentioned them—they upset her, and he was curious.

Once, when he was almost ten, he'd pestered her with questions about her childhood, his grandparents, and why she never discussed them. The conversation ended with his mother crying bitter tears—and still withholding answers. Finn hated when his mother cried, and he couldn't bear being the reason for it. So, he stopped asking. His grandparents and his mother's childhood became taboo topics, just like Finn's father.

He was, then, understandably surprised on the last day of school, when his mother had abruptly announced that he would be spending the summer with his grandparents.

"The whole summer?" Finn asked, disbelieving.

"Yep. They run a boarding house near Abita Springs. They have an extra room for the summer, and they want you to stay with them."

Finn blinked at first, surprised to hear more about his grandparents than his mother ever offered in the past. "Abita Springs? They live that close? Why have we never visited before?"

"It's… a long story," his mother replied softly.

"Is there something wrong with them?" he'd asked, a little worried.

"There's nothing wrong with your grandparents, Finn," his mother sighed. "I had a complicated childhood, and it's hard for me to engage with them. But they've asked before, and it's time you got to know them."

Finn wanted to point out that her response gave him no new information about his grandparents—alarming, considering he would be spending three months alone with them. But he noticed his mother's far-off, thoughtful look, and he knew there would be no point. He would have to wait. And hope that his grandparents weren't serial killers.

"What about the restaurant?"

His mother managed Le Lapin Dansant, and Finn was used to spending his summers helping her.

"I think we'll be able to get by without one under-age worker."

And just a few weeks later, Finn stood outside his mother's car, watching her shift uncomfortably in the driver's seat. She looked tired and lost in thought. When she noticed him staring, she managed a small smile.

He slung his backpack over his shoulder and grasped the handle of his small rolling suitcase. "You're sure about this?" he asked.

"I think you're going to love them, hon. I'm sorry if this seems strange, but I know if you make the most of this time with them, you can learn a lot and have a wonderful summer."

"Okay."

"I love you. Call me later once you get settled in."

"Okay. Love you too."

Finn turned and crossed the arched bridge. The wheels of his rolling suitcase wobbled on the ancient-looking stones. As he walked away, he felt his mother's eyes on his back. So, he took a breath and tried to push away the unease churning in his stomach.

He scanned his surroundings as he made his way up the hill. Though he was born and raised in largely-rural Louisiana, Finn was undeniably a city boy. He and his mother lived in New Orleans, and there had rarely been any opportunity or money for traveling outside the city. As Finn walked among the massive oak trees with rolling branches and sweeping curtains of Spanish moss, he felt like he had entered another world: a world of dense, creeping fog and strange, dark shapes.

When Finn reached the top of the hill, he got his first good look at the property. In front of the house, there was a large pond with a white, wooden bridge stretching to a small island in the center. A greenhouse and a garden sat on either side of the house. The main building looked like a large cottage—the kind found in fairy tales, but bigger. The three-story structure was all rough stone and thatch with a tall, brick chimney. The unusually-wide front door was painted red, and the bronze door handle was shaped like a bird wing.

A hand-painted, wooden sign in the yard read, "The Thin House."

With the exception of that peculiar sign, Finn found the property tremendously inviting. He was taken aback by the feelings of warmth and hominess that came over him as he approached.

Finn was so caught up in the picturesque nature of the house that he failed to notice the large man with the pistol. But then the man waved, and the motion snapped Finn out of his reverie.

The man had a striking appearance, to say the least—he reminded Finn of Santa Claus. He had a white beard and matching long, white hair held back with a leather cord. But the more Finn looked at him, the less he thought of Santa Claus. This man, for instance, clearly hit the gym with the gusto of a much younger St. Nick. He had an expansive chest and wideset shoulders; the muscles in his forearms stretched the rolled-up sleeves of his flannel shirt.

Furthermore, this Louisiana Santa was armed. He stood behind a folding table, cleaning his gun with rags and gun oil. A thick leather gun belt with a holster and several magazine pouches rested on the table. A strange-looking knife stuck out of the belt. Finn thought its handle was made from the polished horn of some animal, but he couldn't identify it.

The man gave Finn a surprisingly kind smile.

"You Fiona's boy?" he asked, running a rag down the length of the barrel.

"Yes, sir. My name's Finn."

The burly man turned his head back toward the house and shouted with a booming voice, "Eleanor! He's here!" Then, he turned back to Finn, holding up hands that were stained with gun oil. "My name is Ezekiel. I'm your grandpa. I'd, uh... hug you or something, but—I'm a bit oily at the moment."

"Okay," Finn replied. He couldn't think of what else to say.

Then, the front door burst open, and before Finn knew what was happening, he was wrapped in a hug that smelled more of cinnamon and baked goods than of gun oil. After a few long seconds passed, the pleasant-smelling stranger pulled back, and Finn got a good look at her. The woman was beaming. She was just a little taller than Finn and very pretty, with long silver hair and a petite, athletic build. He could not have guessed her age. Her face—like the burly man's, the one claiming to be his "grandpa"—was not wrinkled. But it had a charmingly weathered quality.

"Let me get a good look at you. Wow!" the woman said with an earnest smile. "You really favor your mother. Those big eyes are just killing me!"

"You're my grandmother?" Finn asked.

The woman wiped flour off her hands onto a used-looking apron. She cocked her head and seemed to consider the question seriously. The burly Santa Claus stopped cleaning his gun and watched the woman with an affectionate smile.

"I am your grandmother, yes. I don't know if I'm sold on that title, though. I'm thinking 'Nana Eleanor' and 'Papa Zeke.'"

"'Papa Zeke?'" Finn's grandfather raised an eyebrow.

"'Papa Ezekiel' is too much of a mouthful."

"'Papa Zeke' sounds asinine."

"It does not, you're just being contrary."

Finn looked back and forth between his two increasingly peculiar relatives. "Nana Eleanor" was still beaming at him. "Papa Zeke" began reassembling his gun, but a smile lingered in the corner of his mouth.

Finn looked up at his grandmother and managed an awkward smile. "'Nana Eleanor' and 'Papa Zeke' both sound fine," he said. "...I'm sorry my mom didn't come up."

"Oh, it's okay, honey. We understand. In fact, that's something we should probably talk about before we get you settled." Eleanor shrugged off her apron and moved to hold the front door open for Finn. "Let's get you a treat, and we'll have a chat."

"Darlin', are you sure...?" Ezekiel offered.

"Everyone's asleep, it's fine. Come along now, Finn." Eleanor opened the door and led the way inside the house.

Finn followed. The front door opened into an expansive living room with comfortable-looking leather furniture and a large—if rather old-fashioned—television. There was a huge fireplace, and despite it being summer, a fire crackled inside it. The floors were hardwood, but they were covered with a thick Persian rug. Against one wall, a large wooden cabinet with glass doors contained several hunting rifles and boxes of ammunition. What really drew Finn's eyes, though, were the unusual items adorning the walls and ceiling.

A matching pair of ancient-looking Chinese broadswords hung on the wall opposite Finn. The rough edges of the blades suggested they hadn't always been ornamental. Nearby, a glass case displayed dozens of arrowheads and the head of a tomahawk. There were also a handful of old posters on the walls. Finn saw one for a Harry Houdini show and another for a movie called *It Happened One Night*. On a shelf near the door, several crystals pulsed with a faint blue light. Finn also saw a shadow box containing two voodoo dolls, a pair of masquerade masks, and a massive, fully-intact alligator skeleton hanging from the ceiling. The wide mouth seemed to grin down at Finn.

Finn's eyes settled on a simple photograph of a young couple: his grandparents. They were posed as if for one of the Old West souvenir photos taken at carnivals and state fairs, but his grandparents' photo seemed to have better depth and shading than normal. Ezekiel wore a gun belt and a white cowboy hat; Eleanor wore a stylish leather frock coat over a simple dress. He draped his arm around her, and both were smiling slightly. They stood beside the "Thin House" sign out front.

Beside Finn, his grandmother smiled. "Your grandfather's always been a handsome man."

"When was that taken?"

"When we first opened the boarding house," she said. "The dining room is just through here."

Eleanor led Finn into the dining room, where he found a large wooden table piled high with cookies, brownies, and small cakes. She motioned for him to sit in one of the empty chairs, and then she picked up a plate and began stacking it high with pastries. Finn could see the kitchen through a set of swinging double doors that had been propped open.

"I know it's a lot of food, but... well, we are just so happy to have you visit."

"Everything looks delicious," Finn replied with a smile. He had never seen so many desserts in one place.

Eleanor set the full plate of treats in front of him then sat down in a chair next to him, picking up a brownie for herself. Finn thought she looked a little uncomfortable.

"Your house is really interesting," he said. "Where did y'all get all the stuff in the living room?"

"Some of it's from before we started the boarding house, but most of it's come to us from guests. We have an interesting clientele. Which is really what I wanted to talk to you about..." she said. "I don't imagine your mother has told you much about us or this house?"

"She hasn't told me anything. I didn't even know y'all were here in Louisiana."

"That doesn't surprise me," Eleanor said with a trace of sadness.

"It doesn't?"

Eleanor put down the brownie and placed a hand on Finn's shoulder. Her warm, brown eyes met his, but she seemed nervous.

"Finn, this place, this house... it's not what it seems. We're not just a boarding house."

"What do you mean?"

"Our boarders are... unusual," she said.

A blur of chaotic motion burst through the kitchen doors into the dining room. Finn instinctively pushed back from the table as the blur leapt through the baked goods. Cookies and cupcakes cascaded to the floor. The intruder moved so quickly that Finn couldn't tell what it was, but he got the sense of something small and furry. Barely missing a beat, Eleanor's hand shot out into the flying pastries and serving plates, and she plucked the furry figure out of mid-air.

At first glance, Eleanor appeared to be holding a wild rabbit by the scruff of its neck. Brown and white fur rose and fell as the creature inhaled and exhaled. Its ears wriggled as it calmly regarded Finn.

But Finn only noticed those things in passing.

His attention was preoccupied by the antlers protruding from the rabbit's forehead.

Growing up in the city, Finn never had the chance to go hunting. He did have friends who occasionally went deer hunting with their fathers and grandfathers, so he knew from their stories that male deer—"bucks"—with large antlers were highly desirable. They were often scored by the number of points on each antler.

By that classification system, Eleanor held a six-point rabbit over the table.

The antlers sprouted directly in front of the rabbit's ears. Glancing back and forth between Eleanor and Finn, the creature made a puzzled expression, as if trying to understand the sudden halt to its sugar rush.

"What…?"

"He's a jackalope. A Huichol skin-walker left him here," Eleanor said, quite matter-of-factly.

"A jackalope?" Finn repeated, still confused.

"Zeke calls him Chester."

"But jackalopes aren't real."

Eleanor looked at Finn. Then her eyes swiveled slowly toward the strange creature, who looked surprisingly content with being held so unceremoniously. She looked back at Finn and raised an eyebrow. "Are you sure?"

"Not as much as I was yesterday," Finn admitted, staring warily at the creature.

"He's friendly, just don't give him chocolate."

Finn reached out a tentative hand. The jackalope cocked his head curiously. Finn scratched him softly, just behind his ear. Chester emitted a soft purr and leaned his head back, exposing the fine white fur under his chin. It was as soft as down. While Finn carefully petted Chester, Eleanor placed her free hand on his shoulder.

"As I was saying. Our guests aren't what you may think of as normal. In fact, they aren't always—"

A raspy voice called out from the living room.

"Mrs. Blacklock! I'm sorry, but we need to check out a little early. Have to get back home to Indiana."

Finn turned toward the common area visible through the swinging doors. Two figures slowly shuffled into view, and Finn felt his mouth drop open in sudden shock.

The couple reminded him of the tourists he saw in the French Quarter waiting for beignets at Café du Monde. The elderly woman who'd spoken wore khaki shorts and a tropical print shirt. She was accompanied by an equally-old man in matching clothes. They each

13

wore socks with sandals and sported baseball caps that read "Miami or Bust."

And they appeared to be decaying.

Large swaths of skin were missing from their bodies, and Finn could see exposed bones in the man's forearms. What skin still clung to the couple's bones was dull and weathered and had an almost yellow pallor. Finn was horrified to see that the woman's nose was missing and that the man's ears were held to his head with staples.

Their eyes were dull and faded, but their gazes swung toward Finn when they realized that Eleanor was not alone. The woman paused in her exclamation, and Finn saw the corners of her mouth slowly tilt into a grimacing smile. Her grin exposed several jagged, yellow teeth.

"Oh, I'm sorry to interrupt, Mrs. Blacklock; this must be the grandson you were telling us about." The zombie-tourist-woman continued to grin.

Her companion slowly extended a decomposing, skeletal hand toward him, but Finn was paralyzed by the strange situation and made no move to take it. The man smiled politely at Finn, all the same.

"Nice to meet ya, sport! We've heard a lot about you!"

Finn had never been an emotional child. He was not easily unsettled. Since his mother worked long shifts on every day of the week, Finn was often left to his own devices. He matured quickly in many ways, and by necessity, had developed into an independent, often unflappable kid.

He reminded himself of that as his gaze traveled from his grandmother, to the jackalope, and finally to the zombie couple.

Finn nodded politely at the group—and promptly fainted.

⌂

When Finn eventually opened his eyes, he saw an unfamiliar but cozy bedroom. He was lying on a bed with a thick, quilted bedspread, and as he adjusted himself and looked up at the wall, he saw a picture of a little girl holding Chester.

Ezekiel sat at a small wooden desk, a pair of reading glasses perched on his nose. He was deeply engrossed in a worn, paperback copy of *Lonesome Dove*.

Finn stared at Ezekiel until he looked up, smiled at Finn, marked his place, and shut the book.

"You had a bit of a shock there, huh, boy?" Ezekiel removed the reading glasses and slid them into the front pocket of his flannel shirt.

"Y'all run a hotel for monsters." Finn's even tone hid his growing apprehension.

Ezekiel held up a correcting finger. "A boarding house," he said. "Most guests stay long stretches; a few are more or less permanent residents."

"But they are *monsters*, right?"

Ezekiel considered the question. He stood up and moved to sit on the edge of Finn's bed. He scratched his beard and shrugged.

"Well, your grandmother doesn't like that word. Besides, there's only one real monster in this house, and hopefully you'll never see it."

"But those were zombies," Finn said slowly, in the same tone he might have used to explain that fire was hot.

"Richard and Diane are a nice couple who made some poor decisions while vacationing in southern Africa. They haven't really let the experience slow them down, though," Ezekiel explained. "They stop in for a couple weeks every summer."

Finn took a breath, replaying his earlier encounter with Richard and Diane. "They did seem nice," he admitted.

"Most of our guests are nice, and pretty interesting." Ezekiel placed a hand on Finn's shoulder. "While you're here, Finn, you're going to meet people from all over the world. People who have experienced wonders most can't imagine. If you mind your manners and keep a level head, you could learn a thing or two."

Finn nodded slowly. He made himself focus on his grandfather's words instead of the chaotic thoughts bouncing around his mind. He took another long, slow breath and looked at his grandfather.

"I have so many questions."

"You can ask two. Then, we need to go down for dinner. Your grandmother feels guilty, and she's cooked an alarmingly large meal."

"Are the... guests, dangerous?" Finn asked.

"Yes," Ezekiel nodded. "Most of them can be rather dangerous. But that doesn't mean they're bad folks or that you'll be in any danger. I promise, you will be safe here, Finn."

"Why do they come here?"

"Well, besides the delightful company of your grandmother and me, it's a comfortable place for them. Let me ask you something. When you were coming in earlier, did you see the sign out front?"

Finn nodded. "The Thin House."

"That's right. You see, our world ain't the only one. But there are walls between the worlds that typically keep things separate. Most of our guests aren't natural to this world, but at some point, they or their ancestors managed to end up here. And this world is tough on our guests. The forces that separate the worlds make it difficult, sometimes even painful, for non-humans. But there are a handful of places where the walls are thin. Places where the world doesn't weigh down on them. These places are safe-havens that help our guests manage the pain that follows them. That's why we started the Thin House... to give these creatures a place to rest, and to remind our guests that they aren't monsters. Despite what the world may say."

"It sounds kinda creepy," Finn said.

Ezekiel nodded. "It can be creepy, and exciting, and interesting, and much more."

"How did y'all—?" Finn started, but Ezekiel held up a large, callused hand.

"That's enough for now. Let's go get some grub." Ezekiel rose to his feet and motioned for Finn to follow him.

Finn got to his feet. He followed Ezekiel to the door but stopped before exiting.

Ezekiel turned to look at him. He raised a bushy, gray eyebrow. "You all right?" he asked.

"Are there going to be any... guests joining us?" Finn asked.

"Probably just Gareth."

"Gareth?"

"He's a vampire."

"Oh," Finn said. "Of course he is."

And so, without further comment, Finn followed his grandfather downstairs to attend his first dinner with a vampire.

CHAPTER TWO:
THE VAMPIRE

Finn descended the stairs to the first floor. Everything seemed so bizarre, so unbelievable—but he'd seen the zombie couple with his own eyes. He'd run his hands through the soft fur of the jackalope. And his grandparents seemed so casual about the whole thing. They explained their house of monsters as if they were sharing fun facts about a recent trip to Branson, Missouri.

But it was still hard for Finn to wrap his head around the situation. Why hadn't his mother said anything? Did she know that her parents ran a bed and breakfast for the undead? Finn wanted to ask his grandfather more questions, but as he approached the dining room, he heard his grandmother speaking cheerfully, and the conversation caught his attention.

"He seems like such a polite young man. The fainting is understandable, given the circumstances," his grandmother chirped.

The second voice reminded Finn of some of his teachers from school: knowledgeable, capable of turning any conversation into a thought-provoking lecture. "Oh, quite so," it said. "Most humans handle their first foray into the supernatural with much less aplomb. Did you know, when Wellington first crossed paths with a Kapre during his first expedition in the Philippines, he was so shocked that he ordered his men to fire on the creature? Of course, when their bullets did little more than confuse the giant, Wellington invited him back to his camp for brandy and cigars. He later commented that the Kapre offered stimulating conversation, but that the smell was something of an ordeal."

When Finn entered the dining room, he saw a man who appeared to be in his late fifties. The guest was stocky; he had a slight paunch and reddish-brown, curly hair sprinkled with flecks of gray. His wire-rimmed glasses and red cardigan sweater reminded Finn of cartoon librarians and old men who played chess in the park.

He was seated on the far side of the table, but he rose politely when Finn and Ezekiel entered the room.

"This must be the young man in question," he said. Though he didn't extend a hand, he bowed slightly in Finn's direction.

Eleanor moved to Finn's side and put a comforting arm around his shoulder.

"Yep. This is our grandson, Finn. Finn, this is Mr. Gareth."

"You're the vampire?" The words fell out of Finn's mouth before he knew what he was saying.

After his encounter with Richard and Diane, he had steeled himself for this next introduction. But when Ezekiel said he would be meeting a vampire, Finn expected a tall, grave gentleman with fangs and a black cloak, or at the very least, a glitter-skinned teenager with big hair. He had not expected a portly Mr. Rogers.

Finn's blunt question did not appear to disturb Mr. Gareth. In fact, he chuckled and smiled at Finn with genuine warmth and a glint in his eyes.

"Not what you were expecting?"

"Not exactly," Finn admitted.

"Yes, well, the fiend who converted me to my current state of being was a lot closer to the archetype you probably imagined," said the vampire, taking his seat. "But I have never managed to look anything but utterly ridiculous in a cape."

Finn sat across from Mr. Gareth. Eleanor took the seat next to him, and Ezekiel sat at the head of the table. Finn tried to think of something diplomatic to say.

"I don't think anyone besides Batman could look cool in a cape," he offered.

"Oh, are you a fan of the comic books?" Mr. Gareth asked with surprising enthusiasm. Then, his face fell slightly, and he asked, "Or just the movies?"

"I love comic books," Finn assured him.

"Well, have you read—?"

Eleanor held up a hand to interrupt him. "I'm sure this will be a fascinating discussion, but let's start dinner before it gets cold."

"Very well," Mr. Gareth agreed, good-naturedly.

The dinner table was covered with a multitude of mouth-watering dishes: golden-baked potatoes piled high; oven roasted carrots; a fruit tray; a massive loaf of fresh-baked bread next to a jar of dark, amber honey; two different soups, a French onion and another Finn couldn't identify; and an enormous Thanksgiving turkey.

The hearty aroma of the turkey reminded Finn that he was famished. He began to serve himself from the dish nearest him, but when he saw that no one else reached for the food, he stopped.

His grandparents were holding hands. Eleanor turned to him and asked, "Do you mind if we bless the food, Finn?"

"Uh, sure…" Finn said, surprised by the question. Finn had attended church with his mother, but only on a handful of occasions. They never really talked about religion, and he had never seen or heard his mom pray. The request seemed particularly odd, given that they were dining with a supposed vampire.

Finn watched as his grandparents and Mr. Gareth bowed their heads slightly and closed their eyes. Finn bowed his head as well, but he watched, intrigued, as his grandfather prayed.

It wasn't as long or dramatic as Finn expected, his main reference being the evangelists he'd seen on television. His grandfather merely offered a few words of thanks for the food before them and for the company they were fortunate enough to share. The whole thing lasted little more than a minute—but Finn was surprised at the slight feeling of peace that seemed to settle over the room.

As soon as her husband said, "Amen," Eleanor began piling food on Finn's plate. Ezekiel cut the turkey and placed large slices on first Eleanor's plate, then Finn's, but not Mr. Gareth's.

Mr. Gareth served himself a generous helping of the soup that wasn't French onion, ladling it into a bowl. The soup was a meaty, rust-colored broth with a few vegetables floating on the surface. As Finn watched, Mr. Gareth placed his napkin in his lap, picked up a spoon, and began to eat. Finn tried to get a look at the vampire's teeth, but he couldn't see clearly enough to make anything out.

"Vampires can eat regular food?" Finn asked.

"As long as there is a favorable ratio of blood to other ingredients, yes—which is why you had better refrain from this particular dish. Though your grandmother prides herself on concocting delicious meals that meet the demands of my condition, you're unlikely to enjoy it."

"Where do y'all get the blood?" Finn asked his grandparents.

"From the goats, and any deer Zeke gets when he hunts," Eleanor replied.

"It's just animal blood?"

"For the most part," Eleanor said casually. "We got a couple containers of human blood from a hospital, and we keep them around in case a guest is having an emergency. But we haven't used any in a long time."

Finn nodded. He didn't know what else to say. The whole situation still seemed unreal to him, but his grandparents' cavalier attitudes helped.

Then, Finn saw Chester sidle into the room from the kitchen. The strange rabbit-deer hybrid gracefully hopped toward Ezekiel's chair, stopped, and looked up with an imploring expression. Ezekiel passed a biscuit covered in honey down to the creature. For a moment, Finn watched with interest as Chester began to gnaw on the treat—then he turned back to his own meal. He took a bite of a warm dinner roll and tried to think of a good question to ask a vampire.

"Can you turn into a bat?" he asked.

Mr. Gareth dabbed the corner of his mouth with his napkin and shook his head. "I'm afraid many of the abilities displayed by the vampires in popular cinema are entirely fictitious. I cannot turn into a bat, hypnotize young women, or levitate. I also do not find crucifixes or garlic to be particularly vexing."

"So, you just drink blood? You don't have any powers or anything?" Finn asked, unable to hide his disappointment.

"I do have what many would consider enhanced strength, speed, and dexterity. But I have little use for such abilities," Mr. Gareth replied.

"Why?"

"Mr. Gareth is an intellectual," Eleanor said, placing a second helping of turkey on Finn's plate.

"Except at chess," Ezekiel added with a chuckle.

"Your grandfather manages to win one game in thirty years, and suddenly my four hundred years of educational pursuits are called into question," Mr. Gareth huffed.

"Mr. Gareth is a library aficionado," Eleanor added quickly, changing the subject. "He's traveled all over and studied at the world's greatest libraries."

"Really?" Finn asked, surprised. "Libraries?"

Mr. Gareth leaned back in his chair. The bowl that had contained the dark red soup was empty. Finn couldn't help but notice that Mr. Gareth's eyes twinkled when his grandmother mentioned libraries, but it seemed like a peculiar hobby for a creature of the night.

"Oh yes, I've worked at the Imperial Public Library in St. Petersberg, the Malatestiana in Cesena, the Library of Congress in Washington. I worked at both Chethem's and the Bodlein in Manchester and Oxford respectively. In fact, I personally refused to lend a book to Oliver Cromwell in the 1600s. He turned down page corners, I'm afraid."

"So why do you live here?" Finn asked.

"Well, your grandparents' library, of course."

Finn turned toward his grandmother with excitement. "Y'all have a library in the house?"

"We do," Eleanor replied. "It's taken us a while to build our collection, but we love it, and so do the guests. Plus, it runs in the family. My parents owned a library of sorts, and that's where Ezekiel and I first met."

While Finn lacked the travel experience of Mr. Gareth, he was no stranger to public libraries. His favorite was the Rosa F. Keller Library in Broadmoor. He liked all the natural light that settled in the reading rooms in the late afternoon. Since his mother often worked late, Finn had gotten into the habit of going to the libraries throughout the city after school. He would spend hours in a quiet corner pouring over books on mythology, fantasy, dystopian futures, and any comic book he could find. The more Finn thought about it, a summer spent reading and talking to monsters sounded pretty enjoyable.

"Can I see the library?" Finn asked excitedly.

"Help me wash up some of these dishes, and then maybe Mr. Gareth will give you a tour," Eleanor said with a smile, rising to collect their plates.

After helping to clear the table, Ezekiel retired to the living room with Chester, where Finn heard them watching television. Mr. Gareth disappeared, presumably to the library. Eleanor and Finn quickly established a rhythm of washing and drying the mountain of dirty dishes.

"I'm sorry about the shock earlier," Eleanor said as she passed a plate under the soapy water. "Richard and Diane are really sweet, but without any warning, I can see why their appearance might be alarming."

"It's okay. Your guests seem really neat. It just surprised me, is all," Finn replied, taking the wet plate from his grandmother.

"They are neat. I hope you can meet some really interesting… folks while you're here. But I need you to do me a favor," Eleanor said, passing Finn another clean plate.

"Sure," he replied.

"I'm sure your mother wants you to call her tonight? To let her know you got settled in?"

"Yes," he said, drying his plate.

"When you do, can you not mention anything about the guests, or the more unusual things about the house? At least for now?" Eleanor asked, looking a little uncomfortable.

"Okay... Does my mom not know what y'all do?"

"It's a long story, and we can talk about it all soon. But for now, I think discussing that with her would be upsetting. Do you mind holding off? For just a little while?"

"Sure," Finn said. He was a little concerned about holding back details from his mom, but it didn't seem harmful, and he could see the relief wash over Eleanor when he agreed.

"Thanks, Finn. I think you're going to have a wonderful time this summer. Why don't you run along to the library? It's on the second floor, first room on the left."

Finn didn't have to be told twice. He excused himself and quickly left the kitchen, hurrying through the living room where he passed the dozing Ezekiel. Chester was perched on his chest, staring intently at the TV.

Beyond the living room, Finn walked into the wide hallway that led to the stairs. He saw several doors that presumably led to guest rooms, with the stairs at the far end opposite him. Halfway down the hall, there stood an antique grandfather clock that almost reached the ceiling. As he passed, Finn paused and looked up at the clock.

There was nothing outwardly unusual about the antique. To Finn, it appeared rather unremarkable. But as he stood there in front of the clock, the strangest sensation came over him.

He felt something staring back.

Finn frowned and leaned in closer. The timepiece hands weren't moving, and he couldn't hear the soft ticking he expected from a working clock. As he studied the face more closely, Finn felt his strange unease intensify, though he couldn't understand why he felt so uncomfortable.

Despite the peculiar dread creeping up his spine, Finn reached for the face of the grandfather clock. He felt like he was watching himself in a dream. He tried to regain control, to make his body listen to the unease growing within him, but his hand drew closer and closer.

Though he couldn't say why, Finn felt as if he were being inspected. As if he were a piece of meat, and on the other side of the clock, a butcher waited—knife in hand—examining him for any flaws that needed to be sliced away. Unable to stop himself, Finn's trepidation shifted into true panic.

Then something sharp jabbed his leg.

Finn jumped, startled out of whatever bizarre trance had overcome him. He looked down and saw Chester staring up from the floor. Finn lifted the leg of his pants and inspected his ankle, which felt tender. He found some slight redness where the normally-tame jackalope must have poked him with an antler.

He turned back to the jackalope, but Chester hopped past him and waited at the foot of the stairs. He stared back at Finn with an almost impatient expression, as if to say, "Well, are you coming or what?"

Finn took one last look at the grandfather clock then turned and followed Chester up the stairs.

Mr. Gareth waited for him at the top. When Finn cleared the last step, he was quickly herded into the library by the vampires' excited grip, and Chester darted in behind them.

Despite Mr. Gareth's earlier praises, Finn was expecting a large bedroom that had been converted into a library—not anything particularly elaborate. He expected a handful of bookshelves, a table, and some chairs.

Finn was completely and totally mistaken in his assumption.

When he stepped onto the plush, red carpeting, his eyes widened in surprise at the sheer number of books before him. Beautiful wooden bookshelves bordered the entire room and extended floor-to-ceiling. The shelves were packed with hardcovers and paperbacks, with books that appeared ancient alongside surprisingly new books from recent bestseller lists. And in one portion of one wall, a crackling fireplace was surrounded by several overstuffed, leather armchairs that Finn could imagine himself sinking into with ease.

Finn also noticed that the dimensions of the room seemed odd. The door's position in the hallway suggested one small bedroom alongside another, but the interior of the library was sprawling. It seemed to take up the entire second floor.

Finn was distracted, however, when he saw a large portion of shelving devoted to comic books and graphic novels.

"It's truly an impressive collection," said Mr. Gareth.

Finn managed to tear his eyes away from the rows of comic books and turned back toward the vampire.

"Have you read all of these?"

"I've read most of them at least once. I'm currently working my way through one of the first print copies of the *Bardo Thodol*, known in the west as the *Tibetan Book of the Dead*. This will be my seventh time."

"Is that your favorite story?" Finn asked.

Mr. Gareth chuckled thoughtfully, "If you are asking about my favorite *book* in this particular library, then the *Book of the Dead* is certainly a top contender; however, it's only a story in a metaphysical, philosophical sense, and one that by nature of my condition, is rather hard to relate to. If you are really asking about my favorite story, then that's a much trickier question."

"What do you mean?" Finn asked, not bothering to hide his confusion.

"Well, as you surely know, books are merely one of the vessels for stories. Other vessels include films, theatrical performances, songs, even people. In my experience, if the story is truly worthwhile, the type of vessel through which it's conveyed is of little consequence. Good stories find their way to us through many diverse paths. But can I let you in on a secret, young Master Finn?"

"Sure." Finn found Mr. Gareth's soft, lecturing way of speaking almost hypnotic.

"When I tell others that the Thin House has one of the greatest libraries in the world, I'm not referring to this room or its contents," Mr. Gareth said with a smile.

"You're not? I think it's pretty great," Finn replied.

"It is a pleasant personal collection. But if you think of a library as a home for stories, this room is not the real library. The house is. And the stories don't reside between pages, but in the lives of the occupants. My favorite stories, Finn, are those belonging to the creatures that find rest and peace in this place—as well as your grandparents. In fact, if I had to pick an absolute favorite story, it just might be theirs."

"What is their story?" Finn asked, intrigued.

"One of chaos and violence, then peace and order. It is a story about faith, duality, and the nature of real power. But I think when you strip it to its core, theirs is a love story. Unfortunately, it is not mine to tell right now."

Finn was captivated by the new information about his grandparents, but Mr. Gareth offered no further details. Finn thought it would be rude to press him on the subject, so instead, he said, "You must really love stories."

"There is much to love about stories. They teach us, inspire us, and sometimes provide an escape. Which may be the most important benefit, especially in the daunting face of eternity."

"Is that why you love them?" Finn asked.

"Perhaps," Mr. Gareth said, with a trace of sudden sadness. Then, he moved toward one of the chairs by the fire. There was already a stack of books waiting. On top of the pile was an ancient-looking tome with exotic, unfamiliar writing on the cover.

Finn was a little confused by the sudden change in Mr. Gareth. "So what's your story? I'm sure you've had a lot of adventures," he asked, trying to lighten the mood.

Mr. Gareth turned slightly and regarded Finn over his shoulder. Though he still sported his usual small smile, it seemed almost brittle—and for the first time, Mr. Gareth seemed like a genuine vampire. His gaze was ancient, lined with a history that was hard for Finn to comprehend. But there was no malice, only sorrow.

"Have you ever read a book or seen a movie that makes you feel sadness long after it's finished? A story that feels important and meaningful, but is so emotionally raw, that you would never think about revisiting it? One that you are glad you experienced, but would never choose to again?"

Finn thought about books like *The Bridge to Terabithia* and *Where the Red Fern Grows*—books that almost made Finn's throat tighten, just thinking about them. He felt his head nod. He knew exactly the kind of story that Mr. Gareth meant.

"I haven't had many adventures, Finn. I have spent hundreds of years searching for the stories of other people, because my own story is not so easily revisited or shared. My story tells of a loss that, even with centuries of perspective, has yielded little insight, but an abundance of pain."

Finn thought, and then he looked back at Mr. Gareth. "Whenever something bad happens to me, I think about it a lot. If someone makes fun of me, or if I get in a fight, once it's over, I replay it in my head and think about how it could have been different or what caused it. Sometimes that helps, but the thing that always makes me feel better, is talking to my mom about it."

"What are you suggesting, Master Finn?" Mr. Gareth asked.

"I think hearing other people's stories is nice, but sometimes, what people need is to tell their own story. If you ever want to talk about things, I wouldn't mind listening."

Mr. Gareth smiled with real sincerity.

"Thank you. That's very kind, Finn. I may take you up on that offer one day." Mr. Gareth turned back to his book. "But for tonight, I think I prefer to lose myself in Eastern wisdom. Besides, there is a stack of comics by that chair that is calling out your name."

Finn looked at the chair next to Mr. Gareth's and saw a two-feet-high stack of *Batman* comic books waiting for him. He grabbed a couple and slid into the plush chair.

He wasn't sure how long he read before he fell asleep, but he was vaguely aware of Ezekiel carrying him to bed at some point. As he drifted, he found himself thinking of lonely vampires sitting still, distracting themselves with other people's stories. He thought of an old cowboy watching television and a cheerful grandma cooking elaborate meals for a jackalope.

He did not think about strange clocks or feelings of terror seeping through the walls. He didn't think about anything dark or hungry lurking just out of sight.

In retrospect, maybe he should have.

CHAPTER THREE:
THE LAGAHOO

Over the next couple of days, Finn fell into an enjoyable routine. He woke up early and helped Ezekiel tend to the goats, the beehives, and the other chores. Afterward, they enjoyed a hearty breakfast with Eleanor and any guests not on a nocturnal schedule. Once they'd finished breakfast, Finn worked in the garden with Eleanor, and she told him stories about the unusual guests who frequented the Thin House. Then, Eleanor and Finn ate lunch together. In the afternoons, Finn and Chester explored the forest around the house.

Most of the guests slept during the day, so dinner was always exciting. Finn got in the habit of spending an hour or so after the meal talking with the guests. During that first week, he met a trio of harpies, a newlywed goblin couple, a kulam (which Finn learned was a type of Filipino witch), and a girl named Batya who appeared to be just a little older than Finn, but whose vocabulary rivaled Mr. Gareth's. Batya was accompanied by the largest man Finn had ever seen—a man who never spoke, and upon close inspection, appeared to be made of clay. After he helped Eleanor with the dishes, Finn either watched old TV shows with Ezekiel or read in the library with Mr. Gareth.

Before he went to bed, Finn called his mom and gave her an edited account of his day. Though she'd been irritated that he forgot to call on his first night away, Fiona made it easy for him to keep his secrets and his promise. He was surprised to find that his normally inquisitive mother didn't ask many questions about his stay or his grandparents. Their conversations, while pleasant, stayed very general, and Finn found it easy not to go into the supernatural details of his trip. But he always felt a little guilty for not telling his mother everything. He waited for Eleanor to explain why he couldn't share everything with his mom, but she never brought it up.

After speaking with his mom, Finn went to bed, requiring him to ignore occasional wails from the attic. He had not met the ghost who lived there, but his grandmother referred to her as "Ms. Abigail." Eleanor said she mostly kept to the attic. At first, Finn had trouble sleeping, but eventually the soft wails became white noise. Besides that minor annoyance, Finn was really enjoying his first visit to his grandparents' house—eccentricities and all.

One morning, Finn woke up to a gentle prodding. Through sleepy eyes, he registered Eleanor smiling brightly at him. His grandmother wore exercise pants and a tank top, and she held two rolled-up rubber mats under her arms.

"Good morning," she smiled. "I thought you might like to join me for some morning yoga. Interested?"

Finn wasn't much of a morning person, and he was not particularly enthusiastic about waking up to try yoga for the first time. But Eleanor seemed so excited and chipper—he couldn't say no. He nodded in sleepy affirmation and stumbled out of bed.

Finn drowsily followed his grandmother downstairs. In the living room, she pushed the leather sofa out of the way and unfurled the rubber mats.

As she prepped the area, Finn noticed Chester curled up in a small dog bed. The jackalope glanced at him through lidded eyes, then rolled over and went back to sleep.

"Have you tried yoga before?" Eleanor asked.

"No ma'am. My mom goes to a class twice a week, though."

"Well, let's start with a couple minutes of meditation. Find a comfortable seat on the mat." Finn did as she asked; Eleanor sat down, straightened her back, and crossed her legs so each foot rested on the opposite thigh. "This is called Lotus Position."

Finn did his best to replicate the position. But the best he could manage was a kind of tangled, cross-legged… thing. Eleanor assured him it wasn't necessary to copy her perfectly. Finn chose to kneel instead.

"Good. Now, we're just going to close our eyes and breathe deeply. In… and out…"

Finn did as he was told, but he wasn't sure if he was really getting it. He opened his eyes slightly and glanced at his grandmother. Her eyes were closed, and she wore a serene expression.

"So we just sit here? With our eyes closed?"

"Yes, but it's not just sitting. We're trying to clear our minds. Let go of all your thoughts, your worries, and just lose yourself in the breath."

Finn thought about clearing his mind for a moment—before realizing his mistake.

Then he tried to make his mind go blank, to focus on the rhythmic inhale and exhale of his breath. Gradually his thoughts began to fade, and before he knew it, he was lost in his own gentle breathing.

Eleanor placed a hand on his shoulder. "That's enough for now. How do you feel?" she asked.

"Rested… but not groggy. And really relaxed."

"Good. You did great for your first five-minute meditation."

"That was five minutes?" Finn asked, surpised. It hadn't felt that long at all.

"It's a good way to start a morning yoga routine," said Eleanor. "Now, I want to show you some basic poses. Let's start with Warrior Pose."

Eleanor rose to her feet in a swift but fluid motion. She stood up straight on the mat with her palms together in front of her chest, like she was praying. As Finn watched, his grandmother stepped forward with her right foot in a kind of lunge. Then, as she inhaled, she raised her arms high above her head and looked toward the ceiling.

"This is Warrior One. It improves flexibility, but the main purpose is to develop your balance. You try."

Finn replicated the stance as best he could.

Eleanor adjusted his footing then stepped back onto her own yoga mat.

Finn was impressed with his grandmother's flexibility, and he tried to widen his stance like hers. But as he did, he felt a little unsteady. Wobbling slightly, Finn remarked, "You make this look easy."

"You can't focus on flexibility alone," Eleanor said, noticing Finn's shaky attempt at lengthening in the pose. "You have to pair it with stability."

"How do I do that?" he asked.

"Try to connect with the mat through your feet. Imagine weights on your hips, pulling you down into a grounded foundation."

Finn focused on feeling the mat beneath his feet. He imagined them glued to the floor as his legs pressed the weight of his body up. To his surprise, it worked, and he gradually developed a stable base. Once he focused on feeling the ground beneath his feet, a sudden sense of stability came over him.

Eleanor nodded her approval. "That's very good, Finn. Did you notice anything?"

"It seems like flexibility would be really important," Finn said, thinking about some of the contortionist moves his mom did when she practiced at home. "But once I got my feet under me, it felt really good."

"Both are important. If you have one without the other, it's just empty noise. Energy without direction.

Power in yoga comes from pairing flexibility with stability."

Eleanor walked him through several basic yoga poses, and Finn did his best to follow her perfect form. Even though she made it clear that the positions were for beginners, Finn still marveled at Eleanor's grace and strength. After some prodding, Finn got her to show him an advanced form called "Peacock Pose." She did a kind of horizontal handstand, supporting her entire body on just her palms, which were tucked against her abdomen.

Finally, Eleanor asked Finn to show her each of the basic poses she'd taught him. Finn was surprised to find that he remembered them all and, with the exception of Peacock Pose, he was able to perform a passable version of each.

When he finished, she bowed deeply to him, thanked him for joining her, and left to get breakfast started.

Finn still felt very relaxed, so he decided to go read in the library while he waited for breakfast. As he walked upstairs, he wondered how many other kids were doing early morning yoga with their grandmothers while a jackalope slept in the corner.

⌂

When Finn walked into the dining room for breakfast, he was surprised to see a tall, black man with a rakish grin chatting with his grandmother. Finn didn't recognize him, but he was excited to meet a new house guest. He wore a black suit complete with tails and a matching top hat sitting low on his brow. His hands were covered with white gloves, like Finn thought people wore to the opera. One hand grasped a silver-topped cane with strange writing on it. His other hand held a large cigar, which filled the room with smoke and a strange, pungent odor that made Finn feel lightheaded.

But Finn paid little mind to the smell—he was distracted by the man's face. He'd painted a striking, gray-and-white skull around his eyes, nose, and mouth.

The man noticed Finn staring and seemed pleased with the attention.

"Careful with that stare, boy—once folks lay eyes on me, dey have a tough time looking away," the man said in a thick Creole accent.

"Sorry, sir," said Finn.

"Dis y'all's grandson?" the man asked, turning back to Eleanor.

"Yes, this is Finn," Eleanor replied with a smile. She still wore her exercise clothes, but she had a flour-stained apron over her tank top. "He's staying with us for the summer. Finn, this is Kemuel."

"Nice to meet you." Finn extended his hand politely.

"Truly refreshing, to see such good manners in dese troubled times," Kemuel said, taking Finn's hand with a big smile.

Kemuel's hand felt odd in Finn's grip. There was a slight vibration in the man's touch, as if his body were struggling to contain a tremendous amount of energy.

Kemuel quickly released Finn's hand and leaned back in his chair.

"I bet you see all types here, boy."

"Sorry?" Finn asked, confused.

"Monsters! Creatures, otherworldly beings, generally weird folks! I bet you see loads."

Despite his blunt manner, Finn found Kemuel strangely likeable. He nodded and replied, "Yes, sir. But I don't really think of them as monsters anymore. They're our guests." Finn nodded toward Eleanor who smiled approvingly.

"Ha! Hey, dat's a good attitude. I tell you what though, you ain't seen nothing like me."

"What are you?" Finn asked, as politely as he could manage.

The man looked deep into Finn's eyes and grinned. He had unusually white teeth. Finn thought, if they turned out all the lights in the house, they could probably use Kemuel's smile as a reading lamp.

"I'm a little bit of everything."

At that moment, Ezekiel walked into the kitchen, Chester hopping along behind him. Chester honed in on a plate stacked high with chocolate chip pancakes. Eleanor noticed, narrowed her eyes slightly, and moved the plate away from the jackalope.

When Ezekiel saw Kemuel, he stopped and raised an eyebrow. "Kemuel? Didn't know you were in town. You get in just now?"

"Late last night. About to head on. You know I like to ramble."

Ezekiel walked to the sink and turned on the faucet. He placed some soap on his palms and began to wash his hands. Without turning back toward Kemuel, he said, "You know the Baron doesn't like you taking his form. He hears about it, he'll likely make you regret it."

Finn looked at Kemuel with confusion, but the jovial man just laughed. "I ain't afraid of dat ol' fool. Besides, who's to say the look belongs to him?"

As he spoke, Finn saw that Kemuel wasn't a tall, black man at all, but a short, portly Asian man with a long, white beard. Instead of a stylish suit, he wore golden, silken robes, and the cane and cigar were gone—replaced instead with a long-stemmed pipe and a twisted walking staff. A third eye was painted in the middle of his forehead.

"Are you a shapeshifter?" Finn asked excitedly. He had met a handful of guests, but Kemuel would have been his first shapeshifter.

Kemuel turned to Finn, seeming to focus on him with his third eye. Though the guest's form had changed, his voice carried the same rich, Creole accent.

"Like I said, I'm a bit a' everything." As he spoke, Kemuel's ears stretched and came to sharp points; all his features sharpened into harsh angles. His beard receded into his face, and his hair changed from pure white to a fine, pale blond. Finn watched as the man's large belly flattened, and he took on a slim, agile form. His clothes changed from the bright yellow robes of an Eastern mystic to the animal furs and woven vines of a wood elf.

"Kemuel is a Lagahoo, a special kind of shapeshifter from Trinidad," Eleanor said, pushing the chocolate pancakes farther away from Chester. He edged closer.

"Special ain't half of it! We Lagahoos got no rules about changin'. Not just a bat or a wolf, not just durin' one time of the month. I can be anyone or anyt'ing at anytime," Kemuel said, changing again from a wood elf to a large scarecrow with a carved pumpkin for a head.

"So you can be animals, too?" Finn asked, intrigued.

The scarecrow shifted, and suddenly a bear wearing a bowtie sat at the table next to Finn. Finn gasped, and the hairs on the back of his neck stood up. He knew the bear wasn't real, but his body seemed unconvinced. Finn took a breath and tried not to look nervous.

"It seems real," he said quickly.

The bear sagged, and the next thing Finn knew, there was a middle-aged black man sitting at the table. The man wore expensive sunglasses, an exotic looking leather jacket, and designer high-top sneakers. He smiled a familiar, raucous grin at Finn.

"It is real. The trick is, you gotta become whatever the shape is. Lose yourself in the character. I've never been able to fool your grandad, though," Kemuel said, turning back toward Ezekiel, who sat down across from him with a plate of bacon and eggs.

Finn turned to his grandfather. Ezekiel winked at him and passed a bit of bacon to Chester to distract him from the pancakes. The jackalope seemed to sigh, but he took the bacon from Ezekiel in his mouth, munching on it with clear resignation.

"How come he can't fool you? It looked real to me. That bear especially... besides the bowtie, anyways."

"You just got to see clearly," Ezekiel shrugged. "Kemuel can look pretty convincing, but that's just appearances. If you really want to see clearly, sometimes you have to look past the outer appearance. Focus on the heart of what's really there."

"In this case, what's really there is a handsome, debonair citizen of the world," Kemuel laughed, turning back to Finn. "I've been everywhere there is, and done everything you can, all while wearin' a thousand different faces," he bragged.

"Kemuel, are you sure I can't persuade you to stay for a few days? I'll make that Baighan Chokha you like?" Eleanor asked. Finn noted some concern in her voice, but Kemuel waved off the invitation.

"I appreciate the offer, Mrs. Blacklock, but I got to be rolling." Kemuel got to his feet and stretched his back. "I wouldn't mind some assistance with my bag, though. Maybe just to the bridge?"

"I'll help," Finn volunteered. He looked over to the door and saw a large canvas duffle bag with a leather shoulder strap. Finn managed to wrestle the bag over his shoulder while Kemuel and his grandparents said their goodbyes.

"Hurry back," Eleanor called after Finn as he left with the shapeshifter. Finn's grandparents both wore sad expressions as the screen door closed.

"Your grandparents are good folks," Kemuel said when they had walked up the driveway a bit. Despite the sunny day, Kemuel's sunglasses had disappeared. Finn was surprised to see a couple wrinkles around the shapeshifter's eyes.

"Yeah, I'm glad I get to stay here for the summer."

"Enjoy it. These times are precious, and'ey don't last long," Kemuel said earnestly. His leather jacket had vanished, revealing a surprisingly thin and faded t-shirt underneath. Kemuel's arms were thin, wiry, and muscular—the arms of someone familiar with tough, physical labor.

"It's been fun so far. I've never met anyone like you, though," Finn replied, shifting the heavy bag to his other shoulder. "I can't imagine being able to turn into anything like that. Is it hard?"

"No." Kemuel kicked a pebble off the pathway. The dust settled on the shapeshifter's bare, callused feet. He looked at Finn with a pained, tired smile. "It's the easiest t'ing in the world, losing yourself. You spend so much time being something else, it becomes second nature."

Finn remembered what his grandmother taught him during their yoga practice. A shapeshifter probably knew more about flexibility than anyone.

"You wanna know what da hard part is?" Kemuel asked, staring Finn dead in the eye.

"What?" Finn asked.

"The hard part's knowing what you are anymore," Kemuel said, finally turning from Finn. He focused on the stone bridge ahead of them. "I envy your grandad. Able to see da real me," Kemuel laughed humorlessly. "I ain't seen the real me in God knows how long."

Finn didn't say anything. He was surprised to find he felt sorry for the shapeshifter. Kemuel noticed Finn's expression and smiled, sincerely again. He reached out for the canvas bag.

"Don't fret, boy. Ain't nothing for you to worry about."

"I'm sorry," Finn said, handing the bag to Kemuel. Kemuel flipped the heavy bag over his shoulder and let the weight settle.

"Not your fault. Can I give you some advice though?"

"Sure."

"Once you figure out who you really are, don't stray from it. This world's hard on pretenders."

Kemuel gave Finn one last, dazzling smile, then turned and crossed the bridge. He didn't look back.

As Finn stood and watched the shapeshifter go, he tried to look past Kemuel's appearance. He remembered Ezekiel's words and focused on what was truly there. Looking past the worn traveler, he was hit with a strange image: the vague impression of a tall, headless creature trudging down the road. He saw a heavy, pinewood coffin chained to its back.

But more than anything, as Finn watched the strange character depart, he saw confusion and sadness.

CHAPTER FOUR:
THE WEREWOLVES

Finn's favorite pastime at his grandparents' house was exploring the forest surrounding the property. Considering Finn's grandparents' house was full of monsters, myths, and secrets, such an activity might seem comparatively ordinary.

But Finn had always been a city boy. His mother wasn't outdoorsy, so there were never any camping trips. He mostly encountered nature in the small park near his apartment, though it was half the size of his grandparents' front yard and only offered a few trees and some shrubs. So, from the first moment Finn walked the dirt road leading to his grandparents' home, he was transfixed by the trees. He had become obsessed with the towering oaks, with the billowing curtains of Spanish moss that hung from their gnarled, twisting branches, and he was determined to see every inch of the shadowy and seemingly endless forest.

In his first two weeks, he spent hours wandering the ancient, winding trails: the central nervous system of the dense, dark forest. The ethereal woods were a pleasant mystery he meant to solve. He followed strange sounds. He paid attention to otherworldly figures hovering on the edge of his periphery, and he tried to see them more clearly. Far from frightening him, the shadows excited him. Exploring the forest felt like traveling through a dream.

One morning, a dense fog lingered on the ground, and Finn stumbled into a clearing with an old water-well made of thick, roughhewn stones. When he leaned over the lip of the well, he thought he could hear seagulls and waves crashing against a shore. Later that day, he tried to retrace his steps, but he could not find the well again.

Another time, Finn came across a bird's nest that had fallen out of a tree. He picked up the nest with care, working not to jostle the three emerald-colored eggs inside, and placed it safely in the hollow of a nearby tree. The next day, he stopped by to check on them. The eggs and the nest had vanished. In their place, he found a scrap of paper with strange writing on it and a small knife of chipped obsidian with a stag horn handle. Finn kept the knife and showed the note to Mr. Gareth, but not even the studied old vampire could translate the archaic language.

Deeper in the woods, the trails became more complex. They crossed each other, ended abruptly, and occasionally brought Finn to different destinations if walked a certain number of times.

One particular day, Finn determined to find the far edge of the forest. He took the obsidian knife and walked in the most sensible direction. After almost three hours of pushing deeper and deeper through the maze of trails, Finn worried about finding his way back. Ezekiel had recommended marking his way as he went, and Finn berated himself for not listening. He stopped and made an X out of two sticks, deciding to walk for another five minutes and then double back to the X. From there, he planned to return home.

Finn tried to quell the unease rising in his chest, but soon, he changed his mind and decided to make his way home. He passed the wooden X in a rush and backtracked the way he came. He hoped his grandparents weren't too worried; he hadn't expected to be out for so long. After ten minutes, Finn began scanning the woods for familiar signs, hoping to see some indication that he was heading in the right direction.

Instead, he found something that filled him with dread: the wooden X, directly in front of him. He'd gone in a big circle.

Finn groaned and continued on resolutely. He didn't try to backtrack; instead, he walked in a perfectly straight line away from the X.

When he came upon the crossed sticks again after another ten minutes, he finally let himself panic.

Fiercely blinking away the tears fighting their way out the corners of his eyes, Finn sprinted blindly through the forest. He ignored his sense of direction and even the paths themselves, trying to run through the invisible trap he felt clamping down on him. After another ten minutes, a horrified cry burst from his trembling lips.

He once again stood in front of the X.

Defeated, Finn sat down on the ancient, worn path and let his tears fall freely.

But the sound of twigs and leaves crunching underfoot made his head snap up. He scanned the woods but saw nothing. Twigs snapped again, and his hand crept toward the knife. He doubted he would be able to fend off anything serious, but it comforted him nonetheless—until he felt the warm breath of a predator on the back of his neck.

Finn froze, his own breath caught in his throat. He tried to find the attacker in his peripheral vision. When that didn't work, he turned slowly, hoping not to startle anyone or anything.

He found himself face-to-face with a large wolf. It was lean and muscular, with thick, auburn fur surrounding yellow, thoughtful eyes.

Finn tried to control his breathing and stay as still as possible. The wolf stared back at him, sizing him up. It cocked its head to one side and made a soft, whining noise that he found oddly comforting.

"Hello," Finn said nervously, feeling incredibly stupid.

The wolf stepped toward him. He waited for it to pounce, but the creature just walked past him and out of his line of sight. Finn turned his head slightly and saw that the wolf had stopped moving. It looked back at Finn; Finn remained where he was. The wolf made the soft, whining noise again, and he realized that the creature wanted him to follow it. Finn stood and took two tentative steps forward. The wolf turned and began walking down the path at a comfortable pace. Not knowing what else to do, Finn followed the wolf.

After ten minutes of walking, he watched warily for the familiar crossed sticks—but they never came. Even though the wolf seemed to lead him in the same direction he originally tried, Finn began noticing familiar sights.

They were getting closer to his grandparents' house.

Finn kept a watchful eye on the wolf as he walked. Periodically, the wolf turned around and shot him a quick glance. If he slowed, the wolf looked at him reproachfully until he sped up. Finn hadn't spent much time observing wildlife, but he thought the creature moved with an almost unnatural grace for something so large and powerful.

As they got closer to the edge of the forest, he heard his grandfather calling for him. Both Finn and the wolf sped up, and Finn called out in return.

"We're here!" he yelled, including the wolf without thinking. When they reached the edge of the path, he hurried ahead, not wanting his grandfather to panic at the sight of his escort. He waved his hands to get his grandfather's attention.

Ezekiel wore a worried expression and his gun belt as he hurried toward Finn, Chester hopping along behind. Eleanor stood by the front door with an unfamiliar woman.

"You alright, boy?" Ezekiel asked. "You've been gone a long time, we were worried."

"I got lost, but I'm fine now," he said, scratching Chester behind the ears. The jackalope licked his hand affectionately.

"Well, I see you met Eden," Ezekiel said, nodding behind him.

Finn turned, expecting to see the wolf from the forest. Instead, a pretty girl about Finn's age walked out of the woods and smiled at him. She had long, auburn hair and big, green eyes. She was on the pale side, but otherwise, athletic and graceful, with an energetic way of moving.

Finn realized he was staring, and the girl winked at him. He blushed. "You were the wolf?"

"Yep. You got stuck in the loop. I think it's a protection spell or something, right?" she asked Ezekiel.

Finn's grandfather nodded. "That's right. You get too far out, it'll just send you in circles. Only real way in or out is the bridge." Then, Ezekiel looked back at Finn. "I didn't think you'd get that deep. Sorry, boy."

"It's okay. But how come you could find the way out?" Finn asked the girl.

"It's easy to find my way around when I'm all furred up," Eden said cheerfully. "Your grandpa said you'd been gone a while, so I thought I'd find you."

"Thanks," he said, a bit embarrassed that the pretty wolf-girl saw him crying.

"Finn, why don't you show Eden and her mother to a room. I'm thinking the one across from the library," Ezekiel suggested.

"Sure."

"They'll be staying with us for a couple months, so let's make them really comfortable."

As they walked toward the house, Eden introduced Finn to her mother Lahela. Lahela looked like an older, artsier version of Eden. Feathers, beads, and a dried sprig of lilacs were all braided into her long hair. She wore a flowery sundress, sandals made of woven ropes, and big sunglasses. A tattoo of a trail of paw prints spiraled around her upper arm. She introduced herself to Finn with a bright, enthusiastic smile.

Eden and Lahela seemed well-acquainted with Eleanor, who promised them a large dinner of their favorite dishes. They, in turn, looked delighted by the prospect.

As Finn led them through the entrance, he looked back at Eleanor. When Eden and Lahela turned away, a trace of sadness flashed across his grandmother's face. But she saw Finn staring, so she smiled quickly at him, then turned and walked toward Ezekiel.

Finn led the mother-daughter-werewolf duo up the stairs toward the room Ezekiel suggested. The room was simple and cozy, with two beds, a large closet, dual bedside tables, a television, and a private bathroom. A large arched window overlooked the front yard. The view was picturesque, and Finn was surprised when Lahela immediately pulled the curtains shut.

"Can I get y'all anything else?" he asked.

"I think I'm going to have a little nap before dinner," Lahela said. "Eden, if you wanted to go explore some, that's okay. But don't go too far."

"I could show you the library?" Finn offered. "Probably won't get lost there."

Eden laughed and nodded, and they left Lahela to her nap.

The sun hadn't quite set, so Mr. Gareth wasn't in the library yet. Finn gave Eden a quick tour of the impossibly large room, but it became quickly apparent that Eden was already familiar with the library. They walked along the book-lined walls, and she ran her hands along the spine of the leather-bound volumes. She stopped and examined an ancient-looking copy of *Beowulf*.

"Do you like to read?" he asked.

"Yeah, we travel a lot, so I don't get to check stuff out from libraries. But I buy a lot of books from stores and garage sales. I like scary stories a lot."

"Really? What's gonna scare a werewolf?" Finn asked, surprised.

"Most things can be scary, if you let yourself get scared. Sometimes it's fun to go along for the ride, you know?"

"Like watching a scary movie by yourself in the dark," Finn suggested.

"Exactly. I like books and movies I can lose myself in. It's easiest with scary ones, but I like other stuff, too. Your grandmother let me borrow *Pride and Prejudice* last time I was here. It's a love story."

"My grandmother showed me the movie a couple

days ago," Finn said, though he'd spent most of it dozing with Chester. His grandparents watched with the rapt attention of people who'd memorized the film long ago.

"Your grandparents are the sweetest. They love each other so much!" Eden said, a little dreamily.

"I guess," Finn said, but Eden shook her head.

"No, seriously. I've never met people so in love. That's how this place works, you know? Their love spills over and fills the whole house. It's why people like us like it here so much."

"They flirt a lot, for old people," Finn agreed, and Eden chuckled. Then, wanting to change the subject, he said, "I know some scary comics I can show you."

Finn moved toward his reading chair. A stack of comics and graphic novels waited nearby. He was never sure if Mr. Gareth set the books out for him or if the room itself somehow knew what he wanted, but whomever the culprit, he always found a perfect selection ready for him whenever he entered the library.

Finn and Eden sat on the floor by the fireplace reading comics for some time. Whenever one of them would reach a particularly good part, they would stop and share. Eventually, Eleanor knocked on the door to inform them that dinner was ready. Finn and Eden hurried down the stairs together.

Finn was excited to see a dinner table crowded with both food and guests. In addition to Eleanor, Ezekiel, Eden, Lahela, Mr. Gareth, Chester, and Finn, the table included the Reinbecks, a newlywed goblin couple who had been at the house for almost a week; Mary and Ida, twin dwarf sisters who wore axes over their shoulders in leather harnesses; and a tall, thin, redheaded man in a faded green suit who spoke in a thick, Irish accent. Finn once heard Ezekiel call him Red Tom.

Finn loved the nights when many guests joined them for dinner. He loved the peculiar conversations between the boarders. But that night, he was particularly interested in learning more about Eden and her mom. He didn't have to wait very long before Mr. Gareth, true to his nature, provided interesting and useful information.

"Lahela, you will be delighted to know that since our last encounter, I have managed to track down a surviving copy of Gerald of Wales's account of the Ossory Werewolves."

"What are Ossory Werewolves?" Finn asked.

Pleased at the opportunity for discourse, Mr. Gareth removed his glasses and polished the lenses. "The Werewolves of Ossory were a unique breed of werewolves descended from the legendary king Laignech Fáelad. While they were known for their warrior capabilities like their more common counterparts, the Ossory Werewolves were also noted for their compassion, particularly to priests, nuns, and lost travelers. I believe that Lahela and Eden are direct descendants of these noble creatures."

"Well, the lost travelers thing is dead on," Finn said, smiling at Eden. She seemed to appreciate the compliment.

"Mr. Gareth is flattering, but there's really no way of knowing. In truth, I barely knew my mother, much less our family history," Lahela said.

"That may be, but your mother did come from southeastern Ireland, to my recollection. And I have witnessed both you and Eden in your lycanthrope states—you exhibit a control and poise consistent with the legends."

"I don't think an unnatural need to menace cats can be called poise," Lahela laughed. "But that's very kind."

"So, werewolves don't just change during a full moon, then?" Finn asked.

"We *have* to change during a full moon," Eden said. "The rest of the time, it's up to us."

"That's cool." Finn said.

"Sure beats looking like *this* full-time," Mr. Reinbeck said, gesturing toward his gray skin and long, hooked nose as he made a face.

"You're gorgeous, hon," said Mrs. Reinbeck—without a trace of irony.

"I think Red Tom's got it the easiest," Ida said. "He could just not wear green and pass as a normal redhead."

"Nuttin' wrong wit' a bit o' green in the wardrobe," Red Tom grinned.

"Besides, what's a 'normal' redhead?" Ezekiel teased.

Eleanor poked him and rolled her eyes apologetically at Red Tom.

Everyone at the table was chuckling when the howls started.

For a second, Finn thought it was just a dog or a coyote. But then Lahela jolted like she'd accidentally poked an outlet. Finn stared, surprised by her visceral reaction. The howls kept up and seemed to move closer.

Eleanor reached across the table and placed a hand over Lahela's. The other guests shifted uncomfortably, as if they were observing something best dealt with in private—except for Mr. Gareth, who stared at Lahela in sympathy. Chester hopped into Finn's lap and bristled his fur.

Finn turned to ask Eden what was wrong, but he stopped short when he saw that she'd gone pale. She trembled slightly.

"Are you okay? I think it's just a coyote," Finn said, but Eden shook her head.

"No. It's dad... He found us," she said. A particularly deep howl echoed as if from every direction.

Lahela began to cry. Eleanor stood up and hugged her; Mary and Ida moved toward her in unison.

Without thinking, Finn reached out and grabbed Eden's hand. He squeezed it reassuringly, and though Eden seemed slightly surprised, she squeezed back.

The howls stopped. Everyone held their breath. For a moment, it was deathly quiet.

Then, a deep, guttural growl reverberated through the whole house.

"GET OUT HERE, WOMAN!" roared the rough voice.

Lahela flinched, and Eden's shaking intensified. Finn looked toward his grandfather at the head of the table. He was very still, but he listened closely, his right hand clenched into a tight fist.

"NOW! I AIN'T TELLIN YA AGAIN!"

Lahela steeled herself and slowly began to rise, but Ezekiel placed a hand on her shoulder. "You just try and enjoy your meal, ma'am."

He rose to his feet and smiled warmly at her. After dabbing the corner of his mouth, he placed his napkin deliberately by his plate, and then he moved toward the dining room door. When Lahela could no longer see his face, Ezekiel's eyes narrowed, and his smile vanished.

"Ezekiel, don't! It's alright," Lahela said, flustered.

"No ma'am. It ain't," Ezekiel said, stepping into the living room.

Finn saw him approach the cabinet that held the guns. He didn't grab his gun belt, which hung from a hook. Nor did he take one of the rifles from the cabinet. Instead, he opened one of the drawers and pulled out something with a metallic glint—but Finn couldn't get a good look.

"Be careful, babe," Eleanor said steadily.

"Yes, dear."

"He's dangerous," Lahela warned.

"He ain't the only one."

Ezekiel walked to the front door. Chester hopped out of Finn's lap and started to follow along, but Eleanor caught him by the back of his neck and held him snugly. Finn stood up from the table to follow his grandfather too, but Eleanor quickly shook her head.

"No, Finn. You and Eden go upstairs."

Finn started to protest, but then he remembered something, so he just nodded. Eden followed him out of the kitchen, down the hallway, and up the stairs. As soon as they were out of earshot, Finn turned to Eden.

"Do you want to see?"

"Yeah, but how?" she asked. Though she'd been trembling before, her voice was surprisingly steady.

"The window in your room overlooks the front yard. If we open it, we should be able to hear, too."

"Let's do it."

"Are you sure?" Finn asked.

Eden nodded. Her face was a mixture of fear and quiet determination.

They rushed to her room, and Finn went to work on the locked window. The bolt was old and rusted with disuse. While Finn wrestled with it, Eden moved close to the window and watched the scene unfolding below. Ezekiel had stepped outside, but Finn couldn't see anyone or anything else. Finally, the bolt came free, and Finn pushed the window open.

A cool breeze hit them, but they stared down silently as Ezekiel stepped off the porch into the front yard. The moonlight glinted off something metallic wrapped around his right hand. Finn squinted, and when Ezekiel stepped into the center of a bright circle cast by the porchlight, he saw a pair of silver knuckles clenched in his grandfather's fist. Then, a massive shape slipped out of the darkness. The hairs on the back of Finn's neck rose, and Eden's breath caught in her throat.

Since he first met his grandfather, Finn had been surprised by the man's level of activity and strength, especially compared to his friends' grandparents'. One time, Ezekiel asked Finn to help him do some small repairs on the house's emergency generator, which was tucked into a small shed at the back of the house. At first, Finn held the flashlight while Ezekiel tried to work in the small space. But his grandfather became frustrated and decided they needed more room to work. To Finn's shock, Ezekiel simply picked up the two-hundred-pound generator like someone else might lift a bag of dog food. Without much apparent effort, Ezekiel carried the heavy piece of equipment out of the shed and into the yard, where they had more space to complete the repair.

Finn thought his grandfather cut a pretty imposing figure. Ezekiel was always kind and gentle with Finn and the guests, but there was an unmistakable edge that appeared when necessary. With his burly, muscled frame, weapons belt, and intense gaze, Ezekiel often managed to be the most fearsome thing in a house full of monsters. Nonetheless, as the darkness parted and Eden's father stepped into view, Finn felt the first pang of fear for his grandfather's safety.

Eden's father loomed over Ezekiel. Finn thought the man was unnaturally tall, at least seven feet, and he was a mountain of muscle. The man's biceps looked larger than his chest, and his hands were big enough to crush Finn's head like an egg. He wore a dirty tank top, jeans, and big, leather, biker boots. A sleeve of strange tattoos ran down his right arm. His head was shaved, and scars from old wounds covered his face and neck. The big man glared down at Ezekiel, and Finn saw a predatory glint in his eyes.

"If you know what's good for you, old man, you'll march on into that house and bring me my woman."

Ezekiel stared back steadily and said, "Leave."

Eden's father ran his gaze over Ezekiel, appraising him. For the first time, he noticed the silver knuckles on Ezekiel's hand. His eyes stayed on the strange weapon, but he grinned dismissively.

"That jewelry don't scare me, ol' timer. Just gonna get you hurt, when I come show you who the man is."

"Don't talk to me about being a man, cur," Ezekiel said, anger growing in his voice.

"What'd you say?"

"Men don't abuse women and children," Ezekiel growled. "You ain't a man, just some mangy animal looking for something to bite."

Eden's father's eyes narrowed. The grin stayed in place, but his lips peeled back slightly. Even from a distance, Finn could see his teeth lengthen and come to sharp points. "Better watch how you talk to me, chief," he snarled.

"I didn't come out here to talk."

"Old man, I'm gonna tear your head off. Then I'm just gonna walk in and take 'em back with me anyways."

Finn watched in horror as Ezekiel raised his fists, smiling wryly. "Let's see ya try."

Eden's father charged toward Ezekiel. He moved with a speed and dexterity that seemed unnatural for such a large man. From the open window, Finn felt the reverberations of his deep, guttural growl. As he closed the gap between them, Eden's father reached out to seize Ezekiel with his massive, powerful hands.

He was unsuccessful.

Ezekiel deftly slipped to the side and delivered two quick body shots to his ribs.

Finn heard a loud *POP* followed by a crack, and Eden's father winced in pain. His eyes flashed yellow.

Ezekiel followed up with a swift kick to the back of the creature's leg. The larger man sank to one knee and snarled at Ezekiel, baring his growing, animalistic teeth. His right hand flashed out in a quick swipe at Ezekiel.

Ezekiel flinched backward. It looked like Eden's father slapped him, but Finn saw a gash above his grandfather's eye.

Blood dripped from the creature's hand, where Finn noticed a vicious set of claws.

Ezekiel drove his knee into the larger man's groin and followed up with a brutal uppercut that almost knocked the wolf-man off his feet.

Finn wasn't sure what he'd expected from his grandfather, but he certainly had not expected the ferocity on display. With speed and precision, Ezekiel unleashed a flurry of attacks that would most certainly have felled a lesser opponent but only seemed to slow the increasingly wolf-like man.

The only attacks that seemed to do any real damage were the punches from the fist wrapped in silver knuckles. When those blows landed, Finn and Eden heard hideous sizzles and saw small puffs of smoke, as if Ezekiel hit the larger man with a red-hot iron. Gradually, an unpleasant odor of burnt flesh and hair wafted up to their window, and the wolf man was covered in burns.

Despite Ezekiel's efforts, Eden's father kept pressing the attack. He quickly recovered from Ezekiel's assaults, and he did not seem to tire. Ezekiel, on the other hand, breathed hard and slowed. The wound on his forehead bled heavily, dripping over Ezekiel's eye and down into his beard.

Though Eden's father had not transformed into a full wolf shape, as the fight wore on, he looked less and less human. His fingers lengthened, and his fingernails grew into longer and sharper claws. A second row of predatory teeth pushed out over his gums, his face fixing in a vicious snarl. Worst of all, the creature seemed to be getting larger and larger as the fighting intensified. Finn was frightened to see his grandfather look smaller and smaller by comparison.

The wolf-man suddenly caught Ezekiel with a blow that raked across his chest, shredding fabric and skin alike. As Ezekiel stumbled, Eden's father grabbed him in a bear hug and squeezed. Ezekiel groaned as the wolf-man forced the air from his body.

Finn felt his own breath catch at the sight.

Eden placed a reassuring hand on his shoulder.

"I've never seen anyone give him this much trouble," she said. "Don't worry, I think your grandpa's still in this."

Then, Ezekiel slammed his forehead into the wolf-man's face. Blood spurted from the broken nose, and Eden's father loosened his grip slightly. Ezekiel leaned back even farther and delivered another vicious head-butt to the same spot.

The wolf-man released Ezekiel entirely. Eden's father stood dazed as Finn's grandfather delivered a heavy right hook into the mangled nose. The burning silver cauterized his wound with a hiss. Without losing any momentum, Ezekiel ducked behind the wolf-man and wrapped his arms around the creature's waist.

Finn watched with amazement as his grandfather locked his arms, dug his boot heels into the ground, and launched himself backward, throwing the massive wolf-man hard into the nearby stone wall. The wolf-man hit the wall so hard that some of the ancient stones cracked on impact.

The wolf-man groaned, but he didn't rise. Ezekiel got to his feet, slipped off the silver knuckles, and walked toward the werewolf slowly. The creature was just starting to stir when Ezekiel reached him.

Finn's grandfather grabbed the wolf-man by each ear and slammed his head against the stone wall. The man tried to flail at Ezekiel's arms, but Ezekiel held fast and slammed his head against the wall a second time. He repeated his attack until the wolf-man stopped struggling entirely.

Then, Ezekiel released the man's bloody head, letting the wolf-man fall limp. Ezekiel took a breath and leaned back against the garden wall. He seemed exhausted, and his beard was matted with sweat and blood. He let the wall support his weight and struggled to return his breathing to normal. As he did, he looked up and noticed Finn and Eden watching for the first time. Confusion flashed across his face.

At that moment, the werewolf growled softly. Finn and Eden watched, horrified, as the wolf-man—now decidedly more wolf than man—rose to his feet, eyes locked on Ezekiel. Ezekiel took a deep breath and steadied himself as the werewolf took a step toward him.

BOOM!

The gunshot echoed in the night air as a bullet tore through the werewolf's knee, sending him spinning back into the dirt. Finn and Eden watched incredulously as Eleanor stepped off the front porch into the light, the smoking barrel of her hunting rifle trained on the fallen figure.

Lahela, Mr. Gareth, and Chester followed close behind. Mr. Gareth kept a supportive arm around Lahela, who appeared surprisingly steady considering her earlier terror. Chester darted ahead toward Ezekiel.

The jackalope hopped on the wall until he was level with Ezekiel's head, and as Finn watched in amazement, the jackalope nuzzled Ezekiel like a cat.

Eleanor continued on. She stopped just out of the fallen wolf-man's reach, leveling the rifle at his chest. The wounded monster's face was a mask of anger, pain, and a trace of fear, but he froze when Eleanor bolted another round into the gun.

"You're done, you hear me? You're gonna crawl back the way you came, and you're never coming back here. Understand?"

The werewolf glared at her, beginning to look more human. Eleanor raised the stock to her cheek and took aim. The werewolf's eyes widened.

"Understand?" Eleanor asked.

"Yes."

Eleanor's eyes narrowed. She stared at the werewolf with a fearsome intensity that, strangely, didn't seem foreign on her normally-kind face.

Finn watched her as she spoke and realized that his grandparents were a fitting match.

"And if you ever go near Lahela or Eden again, I promise, Ezekiel and I will find you and put you down like the rabid dog you are. Clear?"

The wolf-man nodded. Eleanor's tone and apparent comfort with firearms allowed little room for debate.

Ezekiel shuffled to his wife's side and put an arm around her, motioning for the werewolf to leave.

Chester stayed on the wall and cocked his head curiously at the wolf-man. Eden's father groaned, rolled over, and began to half-walk, half-crawl—back the way he came.

Suddenly, Lahela stepped forward. "Jared."

The wolf-man looked back over his shoulder at Lahela. She stared at him for just a moment before slipping a small, plain ring off her left hand. She looked at the ring once, then tossed it to the ground.

Eden's father glared at the fallen ring. Then, he looked up at Lahela. She held his gaze.

The smallest flicker of sadness crossed the wolf-man's face. But without responding, he scooped up the ring with a clawed, blood-stained hand and continued to crawl away from the Thin House.

Everyone watched the wolf-man until he faded into the darkness.

Ezekiel nudged Eleanor, who took a deep breath and shouldered the hunting rifle. He nodded toward the house, and she followed his gaze until she saw Finn and Eden.

Then she sighed, brightened up, and asked the entire group, "Well, who wants dessert?"

As they all filed back inside, Ezekiel leaned on Eleanor for support. When he passed Lahela, he reached out and gently patted her shoulder.

⌂

Finn's grandfather excused himself to tend to his injuries, but the rest of them gathered in the dining room to enjoy bread pudding and dark chocolate ice cream. Eleanor made sure Chester only ate the pudding—then, she disappeared upstairs, presumably to check on Ezekiel.

No one spoke about Jared or the fight. Instead, Mr. Gareth told a story about a skin walker in Australia who often took the form of a talking dolphin to harass sailors. Afterward, Lahela and Eden also excused themselves, followed shortly by the other guests. Finn was left to clean up the kitchen. Chester watched him do dishes before falling asleep in Ezekiel's chair.

Finn didn't mind being alone. He was grateful for the time to think about the events of the evening. He was still reflecting when he finished the dishes and went upstairs.

As he was getting ready for bed, a soft knock sounded on his door, and Eleanor stepped into the room. Her entrance pulled him from his thoughts.

She wore yoga pants and a long-sleeved t-shirt—some nights, she and Ezekiel practiced yoga and meditated before bed, and she never seemed out of place in exercise clothes. The compression pants and running shoes she often favored seemed like a natural choice for his energetic grandmother.

She sat on the edge of his bed and gave Finn a tired smile. "Never a dull moment, huh?"

"I guess not. Is Papa Zeke alright?"

"He'll be fine, don't you worry," she assured him. Then she took a brief breath. "Listen, Finn, you saw a lot things tonight that need some explaining. I'll let Zeke talk to you about firearms some other time, but for now, I just need you to do two things, okay?"

"Okay."

"First, I need you not to worry. I know that was scary, but you're safe here. I promise."

"I've seen fights before," Finn said, but as he said it, he knew it rang hollow. He'd witnessed violent encounters, but what he saw play out between his grandfather and Eden's dad was something else entirely. That raw brutality felt almost alien. He felt changed by the experience.

"All the same, children shouldn't have to see stuff like that. But it's a fact that many children do... Which brings me to the second thing I need from you."

"What is it?"

"I need you to be there for Eden."

"I like Eden, she's really nice," Finn said. Then, he added, "But she also seems really tough."

"You're right," Eleanor replied. "She's nice, and very tough. But tough or not, this can't be easy for her. She's going to need a friend."

Finn nodded. "How long have y'all known them?" he asked.

"Lahela and Eden have stayed with us many times over the years, when things were... particularly bad."

"So that guy, Eden's dad. He's been like this before?"

"He's never dared come here after them, but yes. He's hurt Lahela many times. And probably traumatized that poor girl."

"Why?"

"He's a cruel man," Eleanor said bitterly.

"No, I mean, why do they go back? If he hurts them, why not stay here? Or somewhere else safe?"

Eleanor brushed a long strand of hair behind her ear and sighed. She looked at Finn, and he could see the sadness she felt for Eden and Lahela reflected in her warm, brown eyes.

"A heart given to the wrong person is hard to reclaim. That's why it's so important to know the difference between genuine love and cheap imitations."

"How do you tell the difference?" he asked.

"Like most things, you look at what it produces," Eleanor smiled. "If a relationship yields hurt, selfishness, or cruelty, it's not love. If a relationship creates peace, happiness, and selflessness, you have the genuine article. Your grandfather and I have been together for a long time, Finn. That kooky, wonderful man has brought me more joy than I thought possible. We are both better people because of our time together.

"I don't know what drew Lahela to Jared. He may have been a different person earlier on. But he has spent the past decade taking all that anger and hate in his heart and poisoning Lahela and Eden with it. I think Lahela tried to hold on in the hopes of reclaiming what she thought was there… and out of the fear he beat into her."

"Will she go back to him again?" Finn asked, worried about the answer.

Eleanor placed a comforting hand on his. She shook her head softly. "I don't think so. Lahela left this time because Jared tried to hurt Eden, and seeing everything tonight, I don't think she'll risk putting Eden in danger again. Her fear of Jared paralyzed her for years, but she loves Eden. And in my experience, love always wins out over fear."

"Seems like guns and silver knuckles don't hurt either," Finn said with a smile.

Eleanor laughed heartily. Her laugh reminded Finn of his mother. Though Fiona didn't laugh often, when she did, it was all-consuming and contagious. She'd lose herself in the laughter, and soon, Finn would be lost as well.

Finn giggled along with Eleanor, even though the joke wasn't that funny. After the violence of the evening, the laughter helped. He felt a tension he hadn't been consciously aware of dissipate and fade away.

Eleanor kissed him on the forehead and turned off the light as she left the room. Darkness settled around him, and the cool breeze from the open window licked at his face.

As he drifted into sleep, he kept thinking about what Mr. Gareth told him that first night in the library — about his grandparents' lives being a love story. He remembered what Eden said, about his grandparents loving each other so much that it spilled over into every aspect of the house.

He still knew so little about his grandparents and the business they ran, but he knew one thing for certain: for a home full of werewolves, vampires, and weird rabbits… there was genuine love in the Thin House.

CHAPTER FIVE:
THE DOMOVOY

Finn made good on his promise to Eleanor.

He and Eden became fast friends in the days following her arrival. Finn thought they balanced each other quite well. While he was quiet and often reserved, Eden was talkative and engaging. Both children were curious by nature, but Finn was cautious. He exercised a good deal of forethought before embarking on potentially dangerous activities. Eden, on the other hand, leapt into adventure headfirst, taking no heed of the potential risks or perils.

Those differences only served to strengthen their friendship. Finn found it remarkably easy to talk to her, and he admired her carefree nature. Likewise, Eden found his thoughtful manner charming, and she took special pleasure in making him laugh and act silly.

Though Finn kept more or less to his established morning and evening routines, he spent his days largely with Eden. Whether they were reading in the library, exploring the forest, or swimming in the pond, his time with her became the highlight of his days.

The pair developed a set of regular pastimes. They particularly enjoyed a game they called "Hide-and-

Scare." One of them hid somewhere inside the house; the other counted to one hundred before searching for the hidden player. Just as the seeker was getting close, the hidden player would try to scare the bajeezus out of the seeker. Anticipating a scare in the Thin House—an ancient labyrinth of rooms filled with monsters—made the effect rather potent.

A typical game of "Hide-and-Scare" could last anywhere from a couple minutes to a couple hours. From the outside, the Thin House appeared rather small for a boarding house, but the interior was enormous. Finn explored the house at length in the weeks before Eden arrived, but she managed to show him hidden rooms he'd never found, including a secret stairway that led directly from the library to the attic.

An exhaustive search of the house could take a long time, especially without the benefit of a werewolf's sense of smell. The games always ran longer when Finn was the seeker.

He'd had to get creative to stand a chance. And creativity meant hiding under a bed in a guest room surrounded by dirty troll laundry.

A troll named Clyde last stayed in the room, and since then, it had not been rented to another guest. Eleanor said that Clyde—though on the large size, even for a troll—was terrified of spiders. He'd panicked one night when he'd seen a spider in the bathtub. In his terror, he caused considerable damage to the entire room. Ezekiel hadn't gotten around to repairs yet.

The troll was so embarrassed that he left without checking out, so his clothes and possessions remained in the room. Finn hoped the rather pungent troll odor would mask his scent from Eden's powerful werewolf nose.

The smell proved difficult for him to endure, however. He tried holding his breath, but whenever he gasped for air, the smell hit him all the harder. He'd hidden for almost an hour, a personal best, when he heard the bedroom doorknob turn. The already-still Finn became statuesque as the door creaked open. He listened to the soft thud of approaching footsteps and tried to make his breathing as quiet as possible.

The bed was partially crushed from the troll incident. In order to fit underneath, Finn wedged himself in, looking up at the broken box spring without any room to turn his head. In his peripheral vision, he saw someone standing near the edge of the bed. Sensing an opportunity to scare his friend, Finn reached his hand out like a shot and grabbed her ankle, releasing what he hoped was a terrifying scream.

"Ahhh!—"

He stopped abruptly, and his eyes widened.

Finn knew he'd been developing other feelings for Eden. He hadn't failed to notice her sweet smile, her slim, athletic figure, or the flutter in his chest when they spent time together. Finn knew exactly what Eden looked like.

As such, he was surprised when—instead of grabbing Eden's lean but powerful ankle—he found himself holding something thick, something covered in coarse, oily hair.

Before Finn could even flinch, the owner of the hairy ankle started screaming.

"Oh God! Spare me, please! I take nuthink!"

Finn's fright stalled when he heard the man's terrified, Russian-accented voice. The screaming continued as he clambered out enough to get a good look at the creature. When he cleared his head from the bed and the worst of the troll odor, Finn looked up to see the owner of the hairy legs and the strange voice.

He was shorter than Finn and stocky, but he didn't have the robust, muscular form of the dwarves. He was on the pudgier side, with long, thin arms and fingers. His ears were large and pointed, but otherwise, he looked like any hairy old man. Though he was bald on the top of his scalp, long, gray hair sprouted from the back and sides of his head, and he had a beard to match. Coarse hair covered his arms and ankles. Though the little man was barefoot, he dressed surprisingly well. He wore green trousers and a matching waistcoat over a white button-up shirt.

"It's okay! I didn't mean to scare you," Finn said, crawling out from under the bed. "I was playing a game."

The strange little man calmed down a bit. His breathing returned to normal, and he produced a handkerchief to dab away the sweat beading on his forehead. He looked Finn up and down in confusion.

"Game?"

"Yeah… it's, uh, kinda like hide-and-seek." Finn paused, remembering something. "Hey, I don't mean to be rude, but who are you? This room's supposed to be empty."

"I Domovoy," he spluttered.

"Why are you in here, Domovoy?" Finn asked.

They were interrupted by the door swinging open as Eden and Chester burst into the room. Eden's eyes narrowed and flashed a strange yellow color. Chester leapt between Finn and the little man and lowered his antlers menacingly.

"Are you okay? I heard yelling," she asked Finn, concerned.

"It was Domovoy," Finn said, pointing at the alarmed creature, who took a step back from the protective jackalope.

"Name is not Domovoy. I Domovoy," the creature said with frustration.

"What?" Finn asked, increasingly confused by the turn the game had taken. But Eden relaxed. Her eyes returned to her familiar shade of green.

"A Domovoy is a Russian house sprite, Finn. They bless or curse houses, depending on how they're treated by the families," she explained. Then, she turned to the creature. "But I didn't think Domovoys could leave their homes?"

The Domovoy looked down and shuffled his hairy feet. "Home is gone."

"A homeless home sprite? Huh." Finn raised an eyebrow. "What are you doing in here?"

"New home?" the Domovoy shrugged.

"...Do my grandparents know you're staying here?" Finn asked. Chester prodded the creature inquisitively with one of his antlers.

Instead of answering, the Domovoy took a step away from the jackalope. Finn cast a sideways glance at Eden, who shrugged.

"I don't think you can stay here without telling my grandparents," Finn said.

"No tell Blacklocks," the Domovoy bristled. "Keep secret."

Finn shook his head. "I'm sorry, I don't want to keep secrets from them."

The Domovoy's pale blue eyes pierced directly into Finn's soul. Then, he grinned, revealing small, pointed teeth. "They have secrets. Dark secrets."

"What are you talking about?" Finn asked.

"You keep secret for me, I tell you secret of house."

"How would you know any secrets?" Eden asked suspiciously.

"Every house has secrets. House talk to Domovoy." The Domovoy turned back to Finn. "We have deal?"

Finn didn't trust him. Anyone who could live comfortably amongst the detritus and troll odor of that room couldn't possibly be a healthy, balanced individual. But at the same time, he knew his family had held things back from him. He'd been living at the Thin House for a month, and neither his grandparents nor his mom had shed any light on the mystery shrouding his family's past.

Ultimately, Finn's curiosity won out.

"Okay, what's the secret?"

"There is evil underneath," the Domovoy said gravely.

"...What?" Eden asked.

"Evil underneath home. Hidden behind clock."

Finn remembered something from his first night in the house. "Wait, you mean the grandfather clock? In the hallway?"

The Domovoy nodded but said no more.

"What do you mean, 'evil'?" Eden asked.

"Old evil."

"What does that mean?" asked Finn.

The Domovoy would not elaborate. Eden and Finn tried asking different questions, but he wouldn't even make eye contact anymore. After a few minutes, Finn scooped up Chester and started to leave with Eden. Before he closed the door, he turned back toward the Domovoy.

"I'll bring you some food, if I can," he said.

He wasn't sure, but as he left, he thought he saw the Domovoy smile.

⌂

Finn's grandparents attended church every Sunday at a small meeting house in the nearby town of

Abita Springs. It was the only time they both regularly left the house. They occasionally left on errands, but those outings were rarely planned. Finn knew they would both be away at 9:00 a.m. every Sunday like clockwork.

Ezekiel and Eleanor hadn't pressed him about going to church with them, which Finn found odd. They had been otherwise consistent about sharing their religion. They all regularly prayed together, and on Monday nights, they gathered in the living room to read from Ezekiel's old Bible before playing a card game or watching a movie. But they never asked him to go to church with them. He'd gotten into the habit of reading in the library while they were away.

That particular Sunday, Finn and Eden had a different plan. They watched Finn's grandparents leave from a living room window. Eleanor noticed them watching and waved goodbye. As soon as they saw Ezekiel's old pickup truck roll over the bridge, the pair hurried to the main hallway.

The house was oddly quiet. Most of the guests preferred a nocturnal schedule, except Lahela, who'd left earlier for a run. She was an avid runner—her morning jogs could easily last for hours. However, the children weren't entirely alone as they stepped into the hallway.

Chester stood at the foot of the stairs.

Finn and Eden ignored the jackalope, however, and walked toward the looming grandfather clock. After speaking with the Domovoy, Finn told Eden about his earlier experience with the clock. She had never really noticed the clock before, but both children were intrigued by the Domovoy's cryptic warning.

"Do you think there's a secret code or something?" Finn asked, inspecting the softly rocking pendulum in the grandfather clock.

Eden placed her small, strong hands on the wooden base and tried to move it gently away from the wall. It didn't budge. She strained a bit harder, but nothing happened. She finally groaned in frustration.

"If I push any harder, I'll break the clock."

"Is it attached to the wall?" he asked.

"No." She shook her head. "It feels anchored at the bottom."

Finn pressed the side of his face flat against the wall, and he looked at the back of the clock, finding a razor-thin gap between the timepiece and the wall. He stepped back to inspect the front of the clock. The hands weren't moving, so he got an idea. Slowly reaching for the clock face, he gently grasped the hour hand and began to turn. Something clicked, and the hour hand stuck at seven. He did the same thing with the minute hand, which clicked into place at twelve. When the time read seven o'clock, he heard a sudden *clank* and the rustle of rotating gears before everything went silent again.

Finn stared in surprise. Eden reached out and pushed the clock again. It slid a couple feet, revealing a small track at the base and a narrow, wooden door made of thick hardwood and painted a deep red. Black writing warned, "Do not enter." An iron ring appeared to be the only handle.

Still a little surprised, Finn reached out to grasp the iron ring.

He felt a sharp poke.

He looked down and saw Chester pushing at his leg, distressed and making a throaty, whining noise.

Eden stepped forward and tried to scoop Chester up, but he nimbly hopped out of her reach and continued poking Finn like a small, furry bull.

"That's weird." Finn stepped back and caught Chester as he started to charge forward.

"You think he's trying to warn us?" Eden asked.

"Maybe. He did this the first night I noticed the clock."

"You think we should stop?"

Finn didn't reply. He looked at the door again.

As he stared at the painted wood, Finn felt that strange pull from his first night in the house. He could sense... something, silently beckoning him closer. The rational part of him recognized the danger, but he also suspected that the answers to all his questions were behind that secret door.

"I want to see where it goes," he said.

Eden shrugged as Finn reached for the door with his free hand. Chester squirmed uncomfortably and proved difficult to hold. So, Finn adjusted his grip on the jackalope, and he grasped the iron ring again. It felt heavy and cold in his hand, but he pulled firmly, and the narrow, red door swung open.

Finn and Eden stared through the open doorway at a dark set of stairs leading down into the basement. A pale, blue light emanated from below. But the faint glow only served to accentuate the darkness, and the children couldn't see clearly beyond the first two steps. Finn turned to ask Eden what she thought, when Chester suddenly bit his hand.

"Ow!" he exclaimed, letting go as the jackalope hopped out of his arms and bolted from sight. Finn examined his hand and saw that it wasn't bleeding, but the unexpected bite from the normally-docile creature unnerved him.

"Are you okay?" Eden asked.

"Yeah. He's just freaked out," he replied.

"He's probably trying to tell us something."

"Are you scared?" Finn asked.

"I'm a werewolf," she smiled. "I'll be fine. I am a little scared for you."

Finn laughed, and some of his apprehension dissipated. He looked at the admittedly foreboding stairway in curiosity, his fingers brushing the handle of the peculiar knife stored in his sweatshirt. He took a deep breath, and he came to a decision.

"I'm gonna go," he said with a steadiness that surprised him.

He didn't tell Eden she didn't have to come, and in turn, she didn't punch his shoulder for the suggestion.

The pair simply nodded at one other, and Finn led the way down the dark, narrow stairway.

The stairs went on longer than made sense. The blue light didn't grow brighter as they descended, but his eyes adjusted to the faint glow. He took the steps carefully, steadying himself against the brick walls as the narrow steps curved gradually. Finn was completely focused on not tripping and falling when Eden grabbed his elbow, and he flinched.

"Finn... Do you smell that?" she whispered.

"No, what is it?"

"Sweat, but it's fresh. And I think I can hear a heartbeat," she said uneasily.

"Is someone down here?"

Eden nodded. "Or something."

Finn didn't say anything. They continued in silence before reaching an arch that marked the bottom of the stairway. The stone was covered with strange symbols and archaic writing. Finn trailed his hand along the inscriptions as he passed through the arch into the main room.

The room was a perfect circle, and the walls curved like a dome. The entire chamber seemed cut directly from the stone foundation. The same symbols that adorned the archway were inscribed on the floor and the walls. The room was barren except for a circular, stone structure in the center.

Finn stared at it. From a distance, it looked like the exterior rim of a stone wishing well. But Finn didn't think many wishing wells were sealed with locked, iron gates. Thick bars extended across the top of the well, and they were covered in the same strange writing, all held shut by a heavy-duty lock.

The symbols set into the floor, walls, and ceiling appeared to spiral out from the well, creating a series of layered sequences in the rune-like script. As his eyes followed the spiraling symbols, Finn found the source of the pale light. Four shelves were set into the curved stone wall at equally-spaced points. Each shelf held a grapefruit-sized crystal. And each crystal glowed with a faint, blue light, pulsing with a steady rhythm.

Eden stepped out beside Finn and surveyed the room. He saw her breath hovering in the air, noticing for the first time that the room was bitterly cold. He was beginning to lose feeling in his fingertips.

He zipped up his hoodie and scanned the room again. There was nothing there except the strange wishing well.

"What is it?" Eden asked.

"I don't know. Do you think that's what the Domovoy was talking about?"

"Nothing else down here."

Finn took a step toward the well. He wasn't feeling the unsettling pull from earlier, only the bitter cold and a gnawing curiosity. The room made him uneasy, but he couldn't stop. His footsteps echoed in the cold silence as he moved closer and closer.

"Is someone there?"

Finn stopped dead in his tracks. He turned to Eden and saw her eyes go wide. Her hair was partially held up with a bobby pin, and he could see the small hairs on the back of her neck rise. Uncertain what else to do, he turned slowly back toward the center of the room. The color drained from his face, and his curiosity morphed into horror.

"Please, is someone there? I need help!"

The voice came from inside the well. Finn shot Eden a look then ran forward. He stopped at the ledge and peered down.

Two pale hands shot up and gripped the iron bars. Finn flinched as a man shoved his face against the gate.

"Help me!" he screeched, sending a surprised Finn stumbling backward.

He heard a guttural growl, and suddenly, Eden was at his side, steadying him. She glared at the man in the well with narrowed yellow eyes. Her lips peeled back slightly, revealing a slowly-growing set of predatory teeth. She held her arm protectively in front of Finn.

"Are you okay?" she asked, still glaring down at the man.

Finn nodded and leaned back over the well to look at him.

He was thin and pale. Finn guessed he was in his forties, with a hint of gray in his oily, dark hair, which was a little on the long side for a man his age. Finn guessed he normally slicked it back, but the sweaty hair was matted over his brow. His face had an angular quality, with high cheek bones and a sharply-pointed nose. Sweat beaded on his forehead, and the lower half of his face was covered in a five-o-clock shadow. He wore a crumpled, blue, pinstripe suit with a distinctly vintage look, a white dress shirt, and a yellow tie. A matching yellow handkerchief peeked out of the coat's breast pocket. Finn thought the outfit might have been stylish and professional at one point, but the entire ensemble looked wrinkled and damp with panic-induced sweat.

The trapped man's eyes were wide and pleading. Waves of terror seemed to roll off him, but his eyes clashed with his expression.

The man was grinning.

And yet, there wasn't any mirth in the smile. Finn thought it wasn't so much a grin as a teeth-baring grimace, an ugly, twisting expression that happened to turn up at the corners. The look seemed frozen on his face. Even when he spoke, he did so through clenched teeth, his voice as panicked as his fearful eyes.

"You have to get me out of here, please."

"What's going on? How did you get in there?" Finn asked, not fully processing the horrifying turn of events.

"I'm just a salesman," he stammered from his bizarre prison. "I knocked on the front door, and I saw some strange-looking people. Next thing I know, some big old man hits me, and I passed out. I woke up down here."

Eden gasped, and the man pressed his face against the iron bars. Finn looked into the well, but he couldn't see the man's legs. The darkness was so consuming that he couldn't get a sense of its depth.

"I don't know how long I've been down here. Please, I have a family."

When he mentioned his family, Finn noticed something flash across his face: a hint of anger and loss, before the terrified expression returned.

Eden's eyes returned to normal, and she peered down at the man with concern. "Are you hurt?" she asked.

"I think I've got frostbite on my foot," he nodded. "There's water down at the bottom, and it's so cold. You have to get me out of here, before they get back!"

"You're saying someone put you down here?" Finn asked.

"Yes, you have to believe me," the pale man spluttered, confusion mixing with the fear in his voice. "It was a big old guy with long hair and a beard. He never said anything, just locked me up in here."

Eden examined the lock. It was old-fashioned and the size of a softball, made from the same heavy iron as the gate. Eden applied pressure to the lock. Finn saw the veins in her arm and wrist strain, and she furrowed her brow. The man in the well watched hopefully, but the iron lock didn't budge.

"Is there a key somewhere?" Eden asked.

"I think it's in the gun cabinet upstairs. Hurry, please!"

Eden turned and headed toward the stairs, but Finn remained still. He stared at the cold, frightened man without blinking. Eden stopped and looked back at Finn.

"Come on, we have to help him."

"He's lying," Finn said, keeping his eyes on the pale man.

"What?" The man looked confused. "No, Finn, you have to believe me. They threw me in here to die."

"No." Finn shook his head. "If you were knocked out at the door, how would you know where the key is? Or that there even is a gun cabinet?"

"He let that slip once when he was feeding me. Look, I know it's hard to accept, but your grandfather has been keeping me prisoner here. You have to get me out."

"How did you know he's my grandfather?" Finn asked.

"Well—" the man started, but Finn interrupted.

"And how did you know my name?"

The pale man said nothing.

"My grandparents are good people. I'm not sure why you're in there, but I know them, and you're lying to us."

The man's face shifted. The humorless grin remained, but all the tension and terror in his eyes vanished. His expression became cruel and mocking. He rolled his head sharply backward and laughed through his clenched teeth.

"I love clever food."

Eden's eyes narrowed, and the yellow hue returned. She moved close and placed a hand on Finn's shoulder. Finn just stared. The man raised his head again and met Finn's gaze. He tilted his head to the side, and the grin widened.

"That's all you are, boy. Food."

Something happened to the man's face. Finn couldn't make sense of it at first. His skin expanded and shrank before Finn's eyes. Something moved under the skin, like insects wriggling just behind his face. He pressed against the bars, and Finn realized for the first time that the iron was slowly burning his skin. But it didn't seem to bother him—he stared hungrily at them.

"Meat. Waiting to be devoured."

"Let's go, Finn," Eden said, squeezing his shoulder.

"Not just yet." The pale man let go of the iron bars with his right hand and reached for his mouth. For a moment, Finn thought he was going bite his own hand. Instead, he grabbed his lower jaw firmly and winked.

The pale man wrenched his jaw open violently. He didn't stop, pulling his jaw lower and lower, until it seemed he would rip it off altogether. Then, to Finn's horror, a mass of black tendrils shot out of the man's open maw. The tendrils were thin and sharp and moved in quick, spiderlike bursts. They shot between the gaps in the iron bars and grasped hungrily for the children.

Three wrapped around Finn's neck, and another two grabbed his wrist. Eden dodged to the side, but one still managed to snag in her hair. Finn tried to scream as the black coils pulled him toward the iron bars, but the tendrils were too strong.

As Finn watched in horror, several small pores formed on the black tendrils. Then the pores expanded, spraying a gray vapor directly into Finn's face.

He stopped struggling immediately.

A wave of utter horror engulfed Finn.

He felt like he was falling headlong into every nightmare, every heart-racing feeling of panic and dread he'd ever experienced. It was as if he were being assaulted by every fearful thought he'd ever had. Far away, he could sense something strong and dark squeezing his throat, but he was completely paralyzed by an overwhelming feeling of terror.

Blam! Blam! Blam!

As quickly as they'd appeared, the tendrils released the children, and Finn saw the grinning man's head snap violently backward as the feeling of terror suddenly disappeared. A powerful arm swept Finn and Eden away, and Ezekiel stepped between the children and the monster.

Finn's grandfather shielded the children, and he held the gun trained on the monster's forehead—which sported three large, smoking holes. There was no blood, but Finn saw something black oozing underneath the damaged flesh.

"Get them out! Now!" Ezekiel shouted.

Eleanor and Lahela hurried down the stairs.

Finn noticed a burning sensation on his neck, and he felt dizzy. Eden caught him as he fell. Eleanor lifted him up and rushed him toward the exit.

As he passed out, the last thing Finn saw was Ezekiel firing two quick shots at the monster—it released the bars and disappeared into the darkness.

The darkness soon enveloped Finn as well, but he could still hear the pale man's laughter ringing in his ears.

⌂

When Finn regained consciousness, he was reclined on the couch in the living room. Eleanor sat on edge by his feet. Eden sat in a nearby chair looking faint, and Lahela dabbed her forehead with a damp washcloth. Ezekiel paced in front of the couch, still wearing his weapons belt.

Finn sat up quickly and looked back toward the hallway. He didn't have a great view, but the grandfather clock appeared to be back in its usual place. When he relaxed and looked around the room again, he noticed Chester curled up in a corner, staring back at him. Everyone seemed concerned, but not frantic.

"What happened?" Finn asked.

"You're safe," Eleanor said, placing a comforting hand on his shoulder. "That thing gives off a poison, but you didn't absorb much. You passed out. But everything is okay now."

"Did it take anything?" Ezekiel asked, before Finn could say anything else. His voice sharp with unmistakable worry.

His tone surprised Finn. His grandfather had been nothing but stoic and competent since Finn met him. Even in the face of the enraged wolf-man, Ezekiel seemed calm and confident.

"Um... No, I don't think so." He started to ask what "it" was, but Ezekiel dropped to one knee and looked him square in the eyes.

"Are you certain? It's crafty. Even the simplest thing can be a tool." His voice was solemn and heavy, matching the unusually somber feeling in the room.

Finn started to answer but froze as a horrifying thought occurred to him. His hand jumped to the pocket of his hoodie, and he was relieved to feel the familiar shape of his pocket knife. For a moment, he'd thought it dropped out when he'd fallen. The only other item he'd taken into the basement was a pack of gum, which was still in the pocket of his jeans.

"I'm sure," he said, relieved.

Ezekiel sighed and sat on the floor beside the couch. He leaned his head against Eleanor's leg, and she ran her fingers through his long, white hair.

"Chester came running up to me in the woods," Lahela explained. "He kept pushing me back toward the house."

"We saw them on our way back from the service," Eleanor finished.

"Who was that? What's going on?" Finn asked, suddenly irritated. He was still weary from the poison, but it was time for some answers.

Ezekiel and Eleanor shared a look. Eleanor nodded slightly, and Ezekiel took a deep breath.

"The Rictus ain't a 'who,' so much as a 'what,'" Ezekiel said gravely. "In the early days, when the world was dark and savage, mankind populated the darkness. They filled the space beyond their campfires with monsters born of dread, hunger, and their secret fears. Those fears were so raw and potent, they took shape. They became the first true monsters. These creatures moved among mankind, feeding off their terror. Until they were finally cast out."

"If they were cast out, why do you have one in your basement?" Finn asked.

"The same thing that makes this place comfortable for our guests creates an entrance for their kind," Eleanor said. "That's the main reason we're here, to protect the gate and keep it from getting loose. We started the Thin House to make something... positive, out of the situation."

Eden sat up and said, "But it looked and smelled like a person. I heard a heartbeat."

"That man you saw is just a suit of clothes for the Rictus," Ezekiel said. "He was an insurance salesman who wandered onto our property years ago. The creature lured him into the basement and crawled inside. We think his body shields the Rictus from some of the protective measures in the basement. It never used to able to reach through the bars..."

"Why's it called the Rictus?" Eden asked.

"A rictus is like a smile or grin, but it's frozen in place. It happens when someone's hurt or scared," Eleanor explained.

"That's the face the man in the well was making," said Finn.

"That's the expression all its victims make. They all die grinning and paralyzed," Ezekiel said. His eyes glazed slightly as he spoke. He seemed lost in a memory.

Finn tried to sit up, and he winced. His body felt sore, and his neck and wrist still burned from where the Rictus grabbed him.

"Easy, Finn," Eleanor said, steadying him. "Just being around the Rictus infects people. Direct contact can kill. Take this." She gave him a piece of homemade bread, producing another piece for Eden.

"I'm not really hungry," Finn said, feeling tired and nauseous.

"Just try a little," Eleanor insisted gently.

Finn took a small bite and was surprised to feel the burning ache subside. The pain in his muscles began to fade as well. He scarfed down the rest of the bread as the nausea disappeared. He looked back toward his grandfather.

"Why didn't y'all tell me?" Finn asked.

"We'd hoped to avoid something like this happening," Ezekiel said.

"The Rictus is powerful and manipulative," Eleanor said. "It's gotten out before by deceit and cunning. We didn't want you to get hurt because you were curious. We thought the best way was to keep it secret."

Finn could understand his grandparents' reasoning. They'd clearly meant well, but even with the best of intentions, their secret had proven dangerous.

A slight movement suddenly caught Finn's attention. He looked up the hallway.

The Domovoy sat on the bottom rung of the stairs. No one else seemed to notice him. As Finn watched, the Domovoy shook his head, almost disappointed. And Finn remembered what he'd said.

Every house has secrets.

⌂

In the darkness below the house, the Rictus had a secret as well.

When Ezekiel asked about anything missing or stolen, Finn was relieved to find nothing had been taken from him.

He never noticed how Eden's hair fell freely.

Indeed, in all the turmoil, a missing bobby pin hardly seemed worth noticing. But deep beneath the foundations of the Thin House, a monster in a human suit rolled a thin metal hairclip across its knuckles.

And it laughed.

CHAPTER SIX: THE AUDITOR

Though the worst of the Rictus's effects faded quickly, a week passed before Finn fully recovered. Eden healed faster, but she still spent the following days watching TV, reading, and generally taking it easy with Finn. Chester often joined them watching TV, and Eleanor reminded them to not let the jackalope steal any of their chocolate snacks.

After that night, neither Eleanor nor Ezekiel spoke about the Rictus. Once, when Finn pressed Ezekiel for more information, Ezekiel explained that speaking about the Rictus seemed to make him more active. He assured Finn it was best to ignore the creature.

Finn had a hard time letting it go. He didn't dare go back into the basement, but he needed answers. The night after the incident, he called his mom and tried to probe her for information, remembering his promise to Eleanor and saying nothing of the Rictus outright.

"Hey hon, how was your day?" Fiona asked.

"It was good. I got into a little trouble, nothing serious though."

"Well, be careful not to make trouble for your grandparents. It's tough running that house. I'm sure they are happy to have you, but they have a lot on their plate."

"Yes, ma'am."

"Are you helping out with things?"

"Yes, ma'am. I try to help out with chores and stuff. Today, I helped milk the goats. Did you ever help grandpa with the goats when you were here?" He hoped to get her talking about her past.

"All the time. There was actually a little one named Adeline who followed me all over the place. Dad would carry her outside every night when I went to bed."

"The goat went inside?"

"I think so. Now that you mention it, it's kind of… fuzzy."

"Huh… Hey, Mom?"

"Yeah?"

"It's really fun here. I want to keep coming here once school starts, okay?"

"We'll have to see if that works with your grandparents' schedule, but I'm fine with it."

"I don't get it, Mom, why am I just now meeting them?"

Fiona remained quiet for a long time.

"…My childhood wasn't all mom's cooking and friendly goats, Finn. They love that house, but… It was never my home. It was everyone's. And when you let everyone in, sometimes you let in the wrong sort."

"What do you mean?"

"I don't want to get into it now. I actually need to get back to the restaurant. Remember what I said though. Not too much trouble, okay?"

"Okay."

"I love you."

"Love you too."

Finn went to bed wondering why every clue led to more mysteries.

One morning, Finn woke up early to help Ezekiel with the chores. When he went downstairs, he was surprised to find Ezekiel and Eleanor sweeping and dusting the living room. Finn chuckled as Ezekiel picked up Chester, ran a dusting brush under the jackalope, and set him back down.

Finn started to ask why they were cleaning so early, but then he saw a bit of movement in his peripheral vision. He tilted his head up and saw Mr. Gareth crawling nimbly on the ceiling, brandishing a dust mop. He grinned down at Finn as he ran the mop over the blades of the ceiling fan.

"Good morning, Master Finn. I'm afraid I've been shanghaied into service at this late hour."

Before Finn could ask anything, Eleanor handed him a broom.

"Would you mind taking over in here so I can get breakfast started?"

"Sure… What's going on?"

For such an old home, the Thin House always seemed spotless to Finn; both his grandparents cleaned the property regularly. However, his grandparents liked routine, and an early morning deep-clean—especially one enlisting Mr. Gareth—was definitely not part of their routine.

"We have a special visitor stopping by today," Eleanor said, stepping through the swinging doors into the kitchen.

Chester shot Ezekiel a withering look, undoubtedly irritated at being dusted so unceremoniously, and he hopped after Eleanor into the kitchen.

"Got to get the place in tip-top shape, boy, upper management's stopping by." Ezekiel ran the dust mop over one of the Chinese Dao swords on the wall.

"I thought y'all were the managers," Finn said.

"Everyone's got a boss, in some form or fashion," Ezekiel replied. "Ours feels it's time for an inspection."

"An inspection?"

"Yup. There's a lot to take care of here. If your grandma or I ever slacked off—well, it'd get real serious, real fast."

"What happens if it doesn't go well?" he asked, wondering what could possibly happen to people like his grandparents, who fought werewolves and played chess with vampires.

"I'm not clear on the particulars." Ezekiel paused his dusting and raised an eyebrow thoughtfully. "But I suppose they'd shut the house down, and your grandma and I would turn to dust."

Ezekiel did not sound alarmed. He resumed his dusting.

But Finn's eyes widened, and he began sweeping rather intently.

Mr. Gareth noticed Finn's anxiety and nimbly descended to the floor beside him. He patted Finn's shoulder.

"Nothing to worry about, I'm sure. It is my opinion that the Auditor has a secret soft spot for your grandparents," he said.

"For Eleanor's cooking, anyways," Ezekiel agreed.

Eleanor called from the kitchen, "Mr. Gareth, I think we can manage from here, if you need to get some rest. Zeke, you need to get the animals sorted out."

Ezekiel handed the dust rag to Finn and left to take feed to the goats and chickens. Mr. Gareth gave Finn a last reassuring pat then disappeared up the stairs.

Once again, Finn found himself left alone with unanswered questions.

He sighed and continued cleaning the living room.

⌂

"An auditor?" Eden asked, skeptically.

"That's what Mr. Gareth said," Finn replied.

They sat at the kitchen table feeding the remnants of breakfast to a grateful Chester. The jackalope's visibly-full belly twitched as he scarfed down a thick slice of bacon. Finn scratched the furry creature behind his antlers.

"I wonder what he is," Eden mused.

"What do you mean?" Finn asked.

"Well, I doubt he's just a human... No offense. And if he has the power to shut this place down, then he'd have to be more than a vampire or something."

"My grandparents are human, though."

"You sure about that?" Eden picked up Chester, who was now beginning to doze off. "I've never known a human that could fight a werewolf with his bare hands. And Mr. Gareth told me once that he's been coming here for almost a hundred years. How old are your grandparents?"

"Add that to the list of things I don't know about them," he admitted.

Both children flinched at the sound of a car pulling up in the driveway. Eden set Chester on an empty seat, and they hurried to the kitchen window. Finn pulled back the curtain and looked out at the mysterious guest.

The black car was nothing special. Finn wasn't interested in cars and couldn't identify the make or model, but he knew it wasn't a sports car or a luxury vehicle. It was old but well-maintained. The Auditor parked it in a small gravel area near the front yard.

Ezekiel and Eleanor walked forward as the driver's side door opened and a man stepped out.

Finn first saw his shoe, a black oxford dress shoe that had been polished brightly enough to reflect the sun in a bright glare. The man who emerged behind it was as neat and professional as the shoe. He wore a black suit, a white dress shirt, and a thin, red tie. Finn thought the creases in the suit pants were sharp enough to draw blood. A handkerchief in his jacket pocket matched his tie. Finn also saw a silver tie pin with an unusual shape, but from a distance, he couldn't tell what it was.

The Auditor was the sternest looking man Finn had ever seen. He was tall and thin with sharp features that demanded no nonsense. His serious, cold eyes were somehow intensified by his thick, black-framed glasses, and his short brown hair was neatly combed with a crisp part on the right side. His movements were precise and purposeful, and as he shut the door to the car, Finn noticed he was carrying a slim, black briefcase.

Eleanor greeted him with her usual cheer, and Ezekiel stuck out his hand. The Auditor shook Ezekiel's hand and nodded in acknowledgement to Eleanor. He seemed cordial, but he didn't return their smiles. He gestured for them all to enter the house.

Finn and Eden fled from the window and pretended they hadn't been snooping. The front door opened, and Ezekiel and Eleanor led the Auditor into the living room. Finn shrugged at Eden, and they went to greet the strange guest.

"Oh, here's our grandson I wrote you about. Finn, allow me to introduce you to the Auditor."

"Auditor Number Seven," the man in the suit corrected, extending a hand for Finn to shake.

Finn shook his hand and was surprised by the Auditor's vicelike grip, which seemed at odds with his thin frame. He stared down at Finn with an expressionless, almost robotic gaze.

"Your name is Auditor Number Seven?" Finn asked.

"My name is irrelevant. Our acquaintance is purely based on my function, which is currently that of an auditor. My assignment is sector seven. No other identification is necessary."

Without another word, the Auditor walked past Finn and into the kitchen. Finn shot his grandparents a look, but they were already hurrying past him.

Finn turned to Eden. "That was weird."

"At least he spoke to you. He didn't even acknowledge me. What's up with that guy?" Eden asked.

"I don't know, but he definitely seems off. What do you think he is?"

"That's the really weird thing," Eden said. "It's like he's not even there."

"What do you mean?" he asked, confused.

"He doesn't have a scent, a heartbeat. There's no body heat coming off him. It's like he's made of air!" she said in bewilderment.

"Well, he doesn't feel like air. His grip was harder than Ezekiel's."

"Let's see what they're talking about," she suggested, nodding toward the kitchen.

Finn nodded, and they entered together.

The Auditor sat at the kitchen table with Ezekiel and Eleanor. Next to him, there was a bowl of honey and a plate stacked with fresh biscuits.

Chester eyed the bowl of honey.

"Occupancy appears to have been consistent since '78, and your customer pool seems to be an even split between recurring and new guests," the Auditor said, reviewing pages from his open briefcase.

"We do have devoted regulars," Eleanor agreed. "Honestly, their positive word of mouth is where all the new ones come from. It's not like we can really advertise."

"The purpose of this site was never intended to be commercial, but your management of the business is to be commended," the Auditor said without enthusiasm.

"I read that *Who Moved My Cheese?* book a while back," Ezekiel said proudly. "It really makes a difference."

"However," the Auditor said with the slightest of edges to his voice. "I notice you allowed unauthorized access to the lower chamber recently."

Eleanor and Ezekiel shared a quick, worried look. The Auditor waited patiently for someone to explain. Finn and Eden each looked at their feet.

Eventually, Ezekiel shrugged and offered, "It was an accident that was taken care of, quickly. No one was hurt, and it didn't get free. Not for a moment."

Finn was unsettled to see his grandfather looking nervous and uncomfortable.

The Auditor fixed Ezekiel with an eerily emotionless stare. Then, he looked down and straightened his papers.

Without looking up, and in the same even tone, the Auditor said, "Of course I am aware that it never escaped. Had it escaped, I would have been notified immediately. And I don't believe I have to remind you what the protocol is at that point?"

"No, sir," Ezekiel said.

"Excellent. Now, our records suggest that you have an unusually high number of long-term tenants. I assume that Ms. Abigail, Mr. Gareth, and your grandson account for three of them?"

"Yes," Eleanor said. "And Eden here, as well as her mother."

For the first time, the Auditor looked at Eden. "Your mother is Lahela Anderson?"

"Yes, sir," Eden nodded.

"Very well." The Auditor made a check mark on one of his papers. He looked back at Eleanor. "But that only accounts for five extended stay guests. What about the Domovoy? He has been here for a month."

"Domovoy?" Eleanor asked, looking over at Ezekiel.

"What Domovoy?" Ezekiel asked.

"He is staying in a damaged room on the second floor. I believe your grandson and Ms. Anderson met him recently," the Auditor said, scanning his notes.

Ezekiel and Eleanor looked at Finn.

Finn looked at his feet and said nothing.

The Auditor sighed softly. "You may discuss it later. The Domovoy staying here long term is only an issue if he tries to bind to the property. That would be a rule violation, and tremendously unwise on his part. Understood?"

"Understood," Ezekiel echoed, still watching Finn.

The Auditor dabbed the corner of his mouth with his napkin and placed it beside his plate as he rose to his feet. Finn hadn't noticed the Auditor eating any of the biscuits, but the plate was empty. The strange man placed his notes back in the briefcase. He removed a clipboard, some papers, and a pen, then turned to Eleanor.

"The biscuits were delicious, but I am ready to survey the property. I would like to start with the attic and progress down from there."

"Of course," Eleanor said, and she and Ezekiel got to their feet.

Ezekiel looked over at Finn and Eden. "You kids stay down here, and don't feed Chester anymore leftovers. He's gaining weight."

"Yes, sir," Finn said, disappointed they wouldn't learn more about the bureaucrat.

As soon as the adults left, Finn turned to ask Eden about what they'd heard. He stopped short when she held up a finger. She waited until they heard footsteps going up the stairs.

"So, you want to find out about the history of the house, right?" she asked.

"Yeah...?"

"I bet there are answers in there." Eden pointed at the Auditor's briefcase on the kitchen table.

"The only thing we know about this guy is that my grandparents, who run a home for monsters, are scared of him... And you want to snoop in his briefcase?"

"Not particularly. But do you?" she countered.

Finn thought for a moment.

A short moment.

"Yup."

Finn and Eden both squeezed into the chair formerly occupied by the Auditor. The briefcase was closed but not latched shut. Finn ran his fingers along the cool leather of the case, took a deep breath, and opened it. Though he'd already witnessed the Auditor pulling notes from inside, Finn was disappointed to find mostly more papers and files. The only surprising item was a small bag of marshmallows.

Eden picked up the bag.

"Who snacks on marshmallows?" she asked with a raised eyebrow.

"I like them in s'mores," Finn ventured.

"Right, but when's the last time you ate just a marshmallow by itself?"

"Can't remember."

"Seems odd."

Finn shuffled through the papers. There were a couple check lists related to inventory and several financial spreadsheets he couldn't understand.

Beneath the loose papers, he found several manila folders. Each folder had a label on the outside corner. The first folder's label read "Escuela de las Siete Campanas." Another read "Lost Prairie BBQ." Finn thumbed through some more, and beneath one titled, "Opossum Trot Funeral Home," he found the folder he wanted.

The file labeled "The Thin House" was not as full as Finn expected. There were only three documents in the folder: a single-page document labeled, "Emergency Audit Report #2,176," a similar-looking page labeled, "Emergency Audit Report #2,182," and several bound pages titled, "Entry Point No. 06: Initial Encounter Report."

"Initial encounter? That's gotta have some answers, right?" Finn asked—but Eden was already reading the first page.

Finn shrugged and read along.

⌂

From the Desk of Agent Seven
Entry Point No. 06: Initial Encounter Report

Having responded to the initial alert in Quadrant No. 07, I hereby confirm that a sixth entry point has manifested in a well north of New Orleans in the small town of Abita Springs, Louisiana. Due to the scale of the event triggering the alert, and as outlined in my assignment specifications, I arrived with the full authority necessary to subdue and contain the Entity. However, upon my arrival, I discovered that the Entity had already been engaged and subdued. Due to the unprecedented nature of this occurrence, I have compiled background information on Ezekiel and Eleanor Blacklock, the two locals involved, and on their encounter with the Entity. This information ultimately pertains to my recommendations regarding the future of this sixth entry point.

Our records indicate that Ezekiel Blacklock was born to Constantine and Evangeline Blacklock. Constantine was a traveling minister who worked primarily among the native tribes in the southeastern United States. Apparently, while traveling on a mission trip, Constantine, Evangeline, and young Ezekiel were attacked by a small Comanche raiding party. Constantine and Evangeline were killed, and Ezekiel was taken captive. Ezekiel spent the next fourteen years as a slave in one of the larger Comanche camps.

Our intelligence suggests that Ezekiel's treatment in the camp was cruel and harsh until he was taken under the wing of the tribe's healer and shaman. The Comanche mystic appears to have shielded Ezekiel from much torment and became a sort of mentor to the young captive. Over time, with the medicine man's influence, Ezekiel was largely accepted into the Comanche community. Our records are unclear, but it would seem Ezekiel gained his freedom through an undisclosed violent encounter, at which point he left the tribe.

Upon leaving the Comanche, Ezekiel wandered for two years before journeying to New Orleans, where he secured employment protecting cargo shipments from river pirates.

Though born in Savannah, Eleanor spent the majority of her childhood and young adult life in the small but developing community of Abita Springs, where her parents owned a successful general store. The family was able to afford a servant, a woman from Barbados named Asha. Our records show that Asha came from a strong family line of island mystics. Asha displayed the ability to alter emotions through cooking, and it is believed her food often had healing properties. Asha appears to have become a second mother to Eleanor, and I theorize that she passed her skills along.

A wealthy family hired Ezekiel to escort them to Abita Springs, which was gaining popularity as a resort destination for the well-to-do. While traveling, Ezekiel expressed an interest in learning to read. He was informed of a general store in Abita Springs that functioned as a community library, with the owners' daughter serving as a sort of librarian.

Ezekiel met Eleanor, and the pair became inseparable. Eleanor taught Ezekiel to read, and he quickly exhausted the contents of her family's makeshift library. In turn, Ezekiel taught Eleanor about hunting, fishing, and tracking, skills she apparently had a natural proclivity toward. The pair's affection and attraction grew; they courted and were soon married.

Shortly after their marriage, Ezekiel and Eleanor noticed other members of the community exhibiting strange behavior. Many suffered from insomnia, night terrors, paranoia, nausea, and paralysis, all of which we know result from proximity to the Entity. These symptoms quickly became widespread, though Eleanor and Ezekiel seemed largely immune.

The situation escalated when tragedy struck a family living on the edge of town. After drinking from a well in the forest, Maximilian Fonchet appears to have gone mad and killed two of his farm hands and a housekeeper. The only survivor of the massacre was Maximilian's daughter, who escaped to town during the violence.

The surviving Fonchet child informed the local authorities of her father's sudden madness. A posse assembled and went to investigate. The citizens of Abita Springs were ordered not follow the posse's pursuit. The townspeople waited for their return, but by nightfall, there was still no sign of them.

Ezekiel had been away on a security job but arrived in Abita Springs as the community was becoming hysterical.

I cannot say why Ezekiel chose to go by himself to investigate the disappearances, and I cannot say why Eleanor chose to take her father's hunting rifle and follow after him. I will not speculate on the motives of these admittedly unusual individuals. I can only share the facts of the events as I understand them, and though the details are hard to fathom, I attest to their accuracy.

When Eleanor arrived at the Fonchet settlement, she discovered the bodies of the farmhands, the housekeeper, and the entire posse. At first, based on the damage to the remains, Eleanor assumed a bear had attacked them. Then she noticed Ezekiel engaged in combat with the Entity.

I believe that upon drinking from the ancient well, Maximillian Fonchet unknowingly allowed himself to become a host for the Entity. When Eleanor arrived, Ezekiel had been engaged with the Entity for approximately thirty-three minutes. His ammunition was spent, and though he was approaching complete exhaustion, he held the Entity at bay with a knife given to him by his Comanche mentor. Eleanor assisted him.

It should be noted that neither Ezekiel nor Eleanor was affected by the paralyzing miasma the Entity uses to ensnare its victims. I have not yet ascertained the source of this immunity.

Between Ezekiel's knife attacks and Eleanor's rifle support, the couple was able to press the Entity into the woods near the entry point. Somehow, they were able to separate the Entity from Maximilian Fonchet—an unprecedented event, by our records—and force the Entity back into the well. Without a host to dilute the entry point's security measures, the Entity could not escape.

Fonchet did not survive the separation. As is often the case, the Entity destroyed its host on exit. I realize, of course, that a separation has never occurred without executive authority. However, the Blacklocks' immunity to the effects of the Entity has never been observed in humans. I believe these two unusual occurrences are linked, though I will not speculate as to their origins or relationship.

I arrived on the scene shortly after the Blacklocks stabilized the situation. A cursory sweep confirmed that the Entity was safely contained within the entry point. As is protocol, I used executive authorization to enhance the containment capabilities of the entry point. With the enhanced seal in place, I approached the Blacklocks and collected the information outlined in this report.

Having witnessed the Blacklocks' abilities under pressure and their affinity for managing the Entity, I exercised my authorized discretion and offered them a preliminary contract with all the necessary adjustments. After some deliberation, they accepted. The terms are largely standard. They are allotted one warning prior to termination and are subject to regularly-scheduled, in-person reviews. They have suggested an unorthodox side venture for the entry site, which will likely require discussion and executive authorization.

Additionally, I can confirm that the nature of this particular site largely mirrors that of entry points two and four. While containment efforts will be required to avoid Entity contact, there is no risk of unpermitted access to exterial planes. As such, precautations against the Deviation are not necessary.

I recognize gatekeeper decisions are typically made in council, and this preliminary offer will require executive approval in order to be finalized. However, it is my personal opinion that the unusual circumstances of this event and of the individuals involved should be the subject of further examination.

Though I am certain I have acted in line with my assignment specifications, I will acquiesce to whatever adjustments are recommended by the executive office.

These remarks constitute my full report. I am available for questioning regarding any points of clarification.

Agent Seven
October 31, 1861

⌂

Finn lowered the Auditor's report and stared in amazement at Eden, who held an empty, plastic bag. Chester had climbed into his lap while he read, and the jackalope looked up at him, waiting.

"I can't believe your grandparents are like, a-hundred-and-fifty-years-old," Eden said.

"I can't believe you ate all his marshmallows," he replied.

"It was a good read, I needed a snack."

"Yeah, well—" he started, but she held up a finger, silencing him.

"They're coming back!"

Finn hurried to replace the papers and folders in the briefcase. He looked at the empty marshmallow bag with dismay, but Eden shrugged. So Finn sighed and returned the formless wrapper to the briefcase. Eden snapped the case closed, and they both hurried to the kitchen sink and started doing dishes. Chester grunted and settled back into the chair.

"I think he's hypoallergenic," Ezekiel said to an uninterested-looking Auditor as they all entered the kitchen.

Eleanor saw the kids washing dishes and beamed. "Finn! Eden! That is so sweet."

Eden and Finn just shrugged, watching the Auditor with rapt attention. The strange man walked directly to his briefcase. Finn held his breath as the Auditor opened the case, but he only paused a moment before depositing the clipboard inside and snapping it shut. Finn and Eden both breathed sighs of relief. The Auditor shot them a sharp look, and then he turned back toward Ezekiel and Eleanor.

"You will have the results of my inspection in two to three weeks."

"Sounds good. Anything else we can do for ya?" asked Ezekiel.

"No, thank you," the Auditor replied.

"Well, let me send you home with some biscuits," said Eleanor. She began piling them into a small Tupperware container.

"That is not necessary," the Auditor said in a flat monotone.

Eleanor took her turn to regard the Auditor sharply. She raised a warning eyebrow. "What on earth does 'necessary' have to do with it?"

The Auditor's mouth remained a straight line, but Finn detected a flash of mirth in his eyes.

"Very well," he said, accepting the Tupperware container when it was offered. He nodded formally at Eleanor, shook Ezekiel's hand, then turned and walked out the front door.

Everyone held their breaths as the Auditor's car started up outside. Finn waited for it to roll past the window as it pulled down the driveway, but it never came. The sound of the car gradually faded until it disappeared altogether.

Finn peeked out the window and saw that the Auditor's car was gone. Everyone gave a collective sigh of relief, including Chester, who hopped into the living room to take a nap.

Ezekiel glanced sharply at the kids. "I don't know what you two were just up to, but y'all can bet we're gonna talk about this Domovoy business."

⌂

Finn took full blame for not telling his grandparents about the Domovoy. Eden excused herself after the Auditor left, and he sat in the living room and spoke with Eleanor and Ezekiel. His grandparents didn't seem mad, just confused, and a little disappointed.

Finn sighed. "I'm sorry, I know I should have told y'all when we found the Domovoy. But I promised him I wouldn't tell."

"Why?" Eleanor asked.

"He told me if I promised to keep his secret, he would tell me secrets about the house." Finn paused and looked at Eleanor. "Look, I'm having a great time here, but I don't get what's going on, and I hate that... Eden and I looked in the Auditor's briefcase. I know y'all are really old and have been running this place for over a hundred years. I know guests like Mr. Gareth have been coming a long time, but somehow, my mom doesn't seem to know? She was raised here, but she seems oblivious to all... this." Finn waved at the oddities on the walls, at Chester, who perked up from his bed in the corner of the room.

Ezekiel and Eleanor shared a long look. Ezekiel sighed and looked out the window. Finn followed his gaze.

The view outside was beautiful. The setting sun cast a golden blanket of light over the entire property. Ezekiel looked sad, and for the first time, a little old.

Eventually, he turned back to Finn. "Your mom doesn't remember the otherworldly bits."

"What do you mean?"

"One of the protections on this place prevents humans from remembering anything supernatural when they leave. Even though your mother grew up here, whenever she leaves the property, her memories are... filtered. She only remembers the normal stuff."

"She's lost her memories of all this... forever?" Finn asked, horrified.

"No." Ezekiel shook his head. "If she returns, she gets her memories back. As long as she's here, anyways."

"But why wouldn't she come back? She acts like she's afraid of the place."

"Something bad traumatized your mom when she was little," Eleanor explained. "When she leaves the Thin House, she remembers that something really bad happened here, but she can't remember what. It makes her not want to come back."

"What happened to her?" Finn asked, afraid of the answer.

"When that salesman got into the basement and got taken by the Rictus, I was in town getting groceries, and Zeke was tending to the animals. Your mother was the only one in the house. That monster crawled out of the basement and surprised her. The Rictus rarely goes straight for the kill. It paralyzes its victims and feeds on them until there's barely anything left. I don't know how long it fed on your mom, but when the goats started screaming, Zeke realized something was wrong."

"I rushed inside and fought that thing with everything I had," Ezekiel said. "Eventually, I got it locked up again. But Fiona was nearly catatonic."

"What did y'all do?" Finn asked.

"We didn't do anything," Ezekiel shrugged. "The Auditor showed up, and he helped with Fiona's condition. The physical aspect, anyways. Couldn't do much for the trauma of it all."

"Your mom recovered quickly from everything except the shock. From then on, every time she left the property, she'd get anxious about coming back. No matter what other good happened here, this place is ruined for her."

"That's why you didn't want me to say anything," Finn said. "She wouldn't have remembered. It would just upset and confuse her."

"That's right. We didn't want to lie to you, or to make you lie to your mom. We just weren't sure how to tell you," Eleanor said.

"So, I'm going to forget everything... When I leave?" he asked. His voice trembled slightly at the thought.

"Not everything," Ezekiel said firmly, placing a reassuring hand on Finn's shoulder. "We didn't bring you here so you could learn about vampires and werewolves. We brought you here because we love you and we want to be involved in your life, boy. Just 'cause you forget some of the details, doesn't mean you're going to lose what's made this experience worthwhile."

"Besides, this isn't your last visit. There are going to be many more, okay?" Eleanor assured him with a smile.

"Yeah, that's true." Finn brightened up, but only slightly.

Ezekiel smiled and stood up. "Now, what's this about reading the Auditor's files?"

"I read about when y'all fought the Rictus the first time." He nodded at Ezekiel. "And how you were raised by Comanche Indians?"

"I wouldn't put it like that," he said flatly. "You shouldn't go through other people's stuff in general, Finn, but the Auditor is probably the last... 'person' on earth you want to rile up."

"I'm sorry... What is he, exactly?"

"We're not entirely sure, and we're under contract not to speculate," Eleanor said.

"I read about the contract a little. But I don't get something," Finn said. "It sounds like the Auditor can beat the Rictus. Why doesn't he just... kill it, or something?"

Eleanor shook her head. "If the Auditor had to dispel the Rictus directly, there would be collateral damage."

"The entire property would be destroyed, and since we're tied to the house, we'd die, too," Ezekiel added.

"The Auditor prefers for regular people to keep the Rictus in check."

"Regular people?" Finn repeated, raising an eyebrow.

Ezekiel laughed. "Well, human, anyways."

They were all quiet for a moment. Finn cleared his throat and looked at both his grandparents.

"I really am sorry for causing any trouble. I love it here, and I'm glad y'all invited me."

125

"We're not worried, Finn. Just please, don't do anything else to irritate the Auditor," Eleanor said.

"…Eden ate his marshmallows."

"What?"

CHAPTER SEVEN:
THE KODAMA

Life at the Thin House moved on.

One morning, Finn went downstairs to help his grandparents with the chores, and Ezekiel was waiting for him in the living room. He carried a duffel bag and slung his gun belt over his shoulder.

"Morning, boy. Grab your shoes and jacket. I got an excursion planned for us."

"Okay, where are we going?" Finn asked.

"I got a range set up in the woods, thought I'd teach you how to shoot today," Ezekiel said. He stepped to the gun cabinet and opened the wooden display doors, withdrawing a small bolt action hunting rifle with iron sights.

Finn perked up even more. "Can I shoot your gun?"

"If you listen good, maybe," Ezekiel replied. "Now hurry up, your grandma wants us back in time for lunch."

Finn laced up his sneakers and pulled on his sweatshirt to protect against the morning chill. He was excited about the prospect of getting away for a bit with his grandfather. Finn had been in a bad mood for the previous few days. The Auditor's recent visit still weighed on him. After they discussed everything, Finn and Ezekiel went to talk to the Domovoy, but there was no sign of him. Finn's grandparents didn't seem particularly concerned. They also didn't seem irritated with him or Eden for snooping. But in spite of things settling back to normal, Finn was having a tough time.

He couldn't help feeling anxious about the impending loss of his memories. He'd told Eden, but she shrugged it off. She said there was no way anyone could make him forget if he didn't want to.

Finn knew he shouldn't waste the last weeks of his summer worrying about it, but it was hanging over his head. He hoped shooting with Ezekiel would take his mind off it.

Ezekiel checked to make sure the hunting rifle was unloaded, then passed it to Finn to carry. The gun had a leather sling attached, so Finn slung it over his shoulder like he'd seen his grandfather do with the larger deer rifles. Together, they left the house and headed for the woods.

Finn had become intimately familiar with the trails weaving through the woods behind the house, especially since Eden had shown him how to keep from getting turned around at the outer edge. But Ezekiel led him to a trail that he'd never seen. The dirt path led down to the base of a steep hill. At the bottom, Finn saw what looked like a clothesline running between two metal poles set firmly into the ground. Several clothes pins were spaced out along the wire.

Ezekiel set his bag down a dozen yards away from the clothesline and began pulling out rolls of paper. He handed several to Finn, who realized they were paper targets. Ezekiel hung the targets up using the clothespins. Finn followed suit until there were ten thick paper targets hanging between the two poles.

"Why is this a good spot for shooting?" Ezekiel quizzed.

"...I don't know?" Finn replied.

"Look at where the targets are, and think. Take your time," Ezekiel said patiently. He began taking cardboard ammunition boxes out of the bag.

Finn looked at the targets again. He scanned the area and his gaze settled on the hill behind the clothesline. Though the path leading to the clothesline was gradual, the hill rose sharply behind the targets.

"The bullets will go into the hill?"

"That's right. That's the first lesson you need to learn about firearms, Finn. Bullets travel. You can't just be aware of what you're aiming at, you have to know what's around it, what's behind it. You have to have total situational awareness before you ever think about pulling that trigger."

Ezekiel pointed at the hill. "Shooting here allows us to shoot from a level position, but the bullets won't just go tearing into the forest. They'll bury themselves in the dirt."

"If the bullets went into the woods, could they go far enough to hit someone on the other side? Like on the road or something?" Finn asked.

"Depends on the gun," Ezekiel replied. "But even if they didn't make it out of the woods, they could still tear up the trees, kill an animal we aren't hunting, or hurt someone just walking along. Don't you and Eden play in the woods? And what about Lahela? She runs the trails."

"I didn't think about that," Finn admitted.

"Proper firearm use requires a lot of thinking, but don't worry. We'll take it slow, and eventually it will all be second nature. Do you have any experience shooting?"

"Just zombie games at the arcade."

"I wouldn't mention that to the Tolberts," Ezekiel advised. "Anyways, we'll start with some basics. Let me see that rifle."

Finn unslung the rifle and handed it to his grandfather. Ezekiel pointed the barrel at the ground and motioned for Finn to observe the gun closely.

"This is a bolt action twenty-two rifle. Twenty-two refers to the caliber of bullet. In this case, it's a pretty small one. It's called a bolt action, because it uses a bolt to load the bullets into the chamber."

Ezekiel grasped a heavy bolt protruding from the right side of the gun and demonstrated to Finn how to lift and pull it back, revealing an open, empty chamber. He then reversed the motion, sliding the bolt forward and turning it down to lock it back into place.

"Pulling the bolt like this allows you to move the bullet from the magazine into the chamber of the gun.

Once your bolt is reset, the bullet is chambered, and the gun is ready to fire."

Finn nodded, and Ezekiel pointed at a tiny black lever to the right of the trigger. Finn watched as he flicked the lever back and forth. Finn noticed that when the lever was flicked one way, a small red dot was exposed.

"This is called the safety. You see that red dot? If you can see the red dot, the gun is ready to fire. If the lever is covering the red dot, the gun won't fire. Remember, red means dead. Whenever you handle a gun the first thing you should do is check to make sure the safety is on, then check to see if there is a bullet in the chamber. Show me."

Ezekiel passed the gun to Finn and motioned for him to repeat the steps back to him. Finn replayed the steps in his head, then repeated the motions back to his grandfather. He lifted the bolt, exposing an empty chamber, then locked it back into place. He pointed to the safety, showing Ezekiel that it was on. Ezekiel nodded his approval and took the gun back.

"Good. But remember, regardless of the safety, or whether a gun is loaded or unloaded, you should always treat a gun as if it is ready to fire. Never play with it, and never point it at a person or thing you don't mean to shoot. Understand?"

"Yes, sir."

Ezekiel showed Finn how to load the ammunition into the magazine and how to attach the magazine to the gun. Then he demonstrated how to properly hold the gun, and Finn had to do the same. Ezekiel observed him and made a few adjustments, pressing the stock more firmly into Finn's shoulder. Then he talked Finn through pulling the trigger, teaching him to firmly press the trigger instead of jerking it.

"Good. Now, do you see the two sets of sights? The rear sights are close to your eye there, and the front sights are at the front of the gun barrel."

"I see them."

"You want to line up those two sights on the target, but focus on the front sights. Try it."

Finn practiced on the leftmost target. He aimed at the bullseye and aligned the sights. He focused so that the front sight was clear and the rear sight was just a little blurry. He could make out Ezekiel nodding in his peripheral vision.

"Feel comfortable? Feel loose?" Finn's grandfather asked.

"I think so," Finn said, surprised to find it was true. He'd been excited to go shooting with his grandfather, but he'd also been a little nervous. His grandfather was just so calm that it seemed to be rubbing off on him.

"Good. Let's try some live ammo."

Ezekiel watched Finn try to load the gun. Finn remembered what his grandfather demonstrated and smoothly loaded eight bullets into the magazine and snapped it into place. He checked again to make sure the safety was on, then looked to Ezekiel for approval. Ezekiel nodded, then handed him a pair of ear plugs. He produced another pair for himself and showed Finn how to put them in. Then he walked to the targets and paced off ten big steps. He dragged his heel in the dirt to mark his position and motioned for Finn to join him at the line.

"Alright, boy, I want you to load a round into the chamber, aim at the center target, and remove the safety. Don't shoot, just tell me when you're ready. Okay?"

"Is it going to kick?" Finn asked. He remembered a friend of his talking about shooting his dad's shotgun on a hunting trip. His friend showed him a small bruise on his shoulder from what he called the gun's "kick."

"No. Some bigger guns have recoil, which we'll talk about another time. This gun doesn't have any, though. It's pretty smooth."

Finn nodded and followed his grandfather's instructions. He used the bolt to load a round into the chamber. With the gun pointing at the target, he gently clicked the safety off. He focused and aimed the sight right at the center of the middle target.

"I'm ready."

"Okay. Now just hold right there and breath with me." Ezekiel inhaled deeply, paused, and exhaled softly and repeated.

Finn kept the sights on target and tried to breath in time with his grandfather.

"Good. In… and out. In… and out. Keep on target, but feel your breath."

Finn caught his grandfather's rhythm and soon felt a peaceful calm spread over him. He could hear his grandfather's voice, but it seemed like the only things in the whole world were his breath, the rifle, and the target.

"Hold this next inhale for a moment, and then pull the trigger as you let the breath go."

To Finn, everything seemed too slow. He could feel the rhythm of his breath flowing in and out. He pressed the wooden stock tighter into his shoulder and focused on the front sight, squared at the center of the target. With his grandfather watching over his shoulder, Finn inhaled, paused, and firmly pulled the trigger.

Pow!

Finn was surprised by the loud crack of the rifle, which reverberated loudly in spite of the ear plugs. He managed to keep the gun pointed down range and carefully pressed the safety back on. With the red dot hidden, Finn raised the rifle up against his shoulder so the barrel pointed harmlessly at the sky. He'd seen his grandfather carry the rifle that way earlier, and he assumed it was safe. Only then did Finn look at the target to see where he'd hit it.

Finn was surprised to see a small hole on the outer rim of the bullseye.

He turned and saw his grandfather beaming at him, and realized he was smiling as well.

"Nice shot!" Ezekiel said cheerfully.

"You were right, it didn't kick or anything."

"Yeah, a twenty-two is pretty kind. Good caliber to start off with. First gun I ever shot was this ten-gauge shotgun my daddy used for turkey. That thing would get my attention now—'bout broke my shoulder as a kid."

"What about your pistol? What kind of bullet does that shoot?" Finn asked, pointing to the handgun holstered at Ezekiel's waist.

"This is a Colt 1911. It shoots a forty-five caliber round. Which is a pretty big bullet." Ezekiel drew the gun and pressed a button by the handle. The magazine popped out the bottom of the gun into Ezekiel's other hand. He passed it to Finn.

"I make those bullets myself," Ezekiel said as Finn inspected the magazine. Seven bullets were stacked in the metal tube. Instead of the copper color of the twenty-two rounds, Finn noticed that the forty-fives were silver. Something caught his eye and, peering closer, he saw several strange markings etched into the bullets.

"What's this?"

"Couldn't tell ya. The Auditor drew those markings in the basement to help contain the Rictus. I tried etching them into the bullets. Seems to make them more effective against otherworldly stuff."

Finn passed the magazine back to his grandfather. Ezekiel slid it back into the gun and holstered the weapon.

"Do you carry that gun in case one of the guests ends up being bad?"

"No." Ezekiel shook his head. "None of the guests have ever given us enough trouble to require anything like that. This is almost exclusively for the Rictus."

"Can I shoot that one?" Finn asked.

"Not today. But eventually, once you've got some fundamentals down."

"When you shot the Rictus in the basement, you were so quick."

Ezekiel shrugged. "I'm fair, I guess. I've been doing this a while. With time and practice, anyone can shoot like that."

"Can you show me?"

"Show you what?"

"How fast you can shoot," Finn replied.

"I think you want me to show off a bit," Ezekiel grinned.

Finn just shrugged then looked at Ezekiel imploringly.

"Alright, but only once, then it's back to practice," Ezekiel agreed. He shrugged off his coat and rolled up his sleeves. He motioned for Finn to step behind him, and Finn quickly obeyed. Ezekiel squared himself to the targets and narrowed his eyes.

"You ready?" he asked, staring steadily at the target.

"Yeah," Finn said, excited.

"Alright, watch closely." Ezekiel stared intensely at the target and inhaled deeply through his nose. Finn waited expectantly, but he was surprised when Ezekiel turned back toward him without drawing his gun. Ezekiel raised his eyebrows questioningly.

"Not too bad huh?" he asked.

"What? You didn't shoot yet "

"Boy, I told you to watch closely. I'm pretty quick. You must have missed it," Ezekiel said, shaking his head with a tut-tut.

Finn looked at the targets and only saw the single hole from his shot.

"None of the targets have been hit," he said accusingly.

"What are you talking about? I shot clean through the hole where you shot," Ezekiel retorted.

"No, you didn't," Finn said, shaking his head incredulously.

"Did so."

"Do it again on a different target," Finn challenged.

"I said I was only going to do it once," Ezekiel replied with a small smile.

"It didn't even make a noise when you 'shot,'" Finn said, making air quotes.

"Nonsense. You just got your ear plugs too tight. Anyways, let's get back to your practice."

Ezekiel watched Finn shoot two whole boxes of ammunition. He showed Finn how to shoot while standing, kneeling, and lying flat. He taught him how to move back and forth between multiple targets. He demonstrated how to eject an empty magazine quickly and load a new one. Eventually, he observed while Finn stretched out and tried shooting from farther and farther distances. After a couple hours, Finn found he'd become pretty confident with the small rifle. Eventually, Ezekiel signaled for him to return the gun to safety and remove his ear plugs.

"Great job! I think that's enough for today, boy. Let me show you how to break that gun down and clean it, then we'll head back."

"Okay," Finn said. He watched as Ezekiel disassembled the small gun, laying the parts out on a large towel he produced from his shooting bag. He also brought out a rag, some oil, and a small pocket knife he used to chip off carbon buildup. Ezekiel demonstrated how to clean each part and then watched as Finn did the actual cleaning.

"Cleaning the gun after you use it is an important way to show respect," Ezekiel said as Finn wiped down the barrel.

"Respect for the gun?" Finn asked.

"Yup. Not being respectful of a firearm is a good way to get yourself or someone close to you hurt."

"One of my teachers told us that people shouldn't have guns. She said they make it easy for people to kill. But my friend Andrew's dad told us that good people with guns make the world safer."

Ezekiel shrugged slightly.

"What do you think?" Finn asked.

"Well. Both have valid points, but I think they both miss the mark a bit."

"How do you mean?"

"Well, your teacher is right. Killing is easy with guns. An evil man with a gun can do a lot more harm with a gun than with a rock or a club, and your friend's dad is wrong to think that just being a good person means you can't cause a lot of hurt. Every year, good people with guns have accidents. I read about a guy the other day who tried to stop a robbery with a concealed pistol. He shot the robber, but the bullet passed through the bad guy and hit a bystander in the background."

"Whoa," Finn said, surprised.

"Yeah. Good intentions alone don't count for much. Guns are tools, Finn. They require training, practice, and awareness, and when you combine those qualities in the hands of a good person... Well, then a gun can help accomplish something worthwhile."

"Like what?" Finn asked.

"Like protecting yourself or others from someone physically stronger than you," Ezekiel replied. "When your grandmother stopped Eden's dad a couple of weeks back, she used a rifle to back him down. Your grandmother is an impressive woman, Finn, but she would have been no match for that monster in a fist fight. They used to have a saying, 'God created men. Sam Colt made them equal.' Meaning, guns can be operated by anyone, regardless of size or strength. They level the field to an extent, allowing folks to protect themselves, who might otherwise not be able."

"That makes sense," Finn agreed.

Ezekiel nodded but didn't say anything. He looked off for moment and seemed to be lost in thought. Finn waited. Eventually, Ezekiel turned and looked him in the eye.

"I've seen a lot of violence in my life, Finn. Savagery, destruction, cruelty. It was worse when Elle and I were coming up, but the world changes slowly, and there's a long road still to travel. I hope I live to see a day when the swords are beaten into ploughshares, when the only use for my guns is impressing grandkids with some trick shooting. But until that day, I believe good, capable folks have a responsibility to be ready."

"Ready for what?"

"To answer evil's challenge. To meet it head on and draw a hard line."

Finn looked at his shoes. His voice caught as he spoke. "I don't think I'll ever be ready."

Ezekiel raised a white, bushy eyebrow in confusion. "Why do you say that?"

Hot tears fought their way out the corners of his eyes. He felt himself blush, and he kept his gaze down so Ezekiel wouldn't see, but he couldn't stop the waves of fear and sadness crashing over him.

"I'm not going to remember any of this. You said when I leave, I'm going to forget."

"It's not like—"

"Shooting, yoga, all the stuff the guests have told me. I'm not going to remember any of it. I'll be just like I was when I got here... I won't know *anything*."

"Finn..." Ezekiel reached for his shoulder, but Finn wiped his face and took a step back. He turned away from his grandfather, embarrassed by his tears but angry at the unfairness of it all.

"I just need to take a walk. I'll meet you back at the house." Without another word, Finn hurried away from Ezekiel. His grandfather watched him go and sighed sadly.

⌂

His tears ran freely as he hurried deeper into the woods, away from his grandfather. The farther he ran, the more his sorrow gave way to an anger with no clear target. He didn't blame his grandparents for living there, or his mother for sending him to the Thin House in the first place. He didn't even really blame the Auditor, who seemed in charge of the memory-altering security measures. Finn understood the dangers posed by the house and the need for protecting the guests' secrets. But the idea of losing everything he'd learned — all of Mr. Gareth's stories, all the time spent with Eden — it was just too much.

Finn stumbled to a stop and doubled over, trying to catch his breath. He clenched his eyes shut to stem the flow of tears and balled his hands into tight fists.

Eventually, he straightened up and scanned his surroundings. He was in the clearing behind the house where Ezekiel chopped wood. His grandfather's axe leaned against a massive oak log. The axe had a polished hardwood handle and a leather cord wrapped around the base for a makeshift grip.

Finn hefted the axe, surprised at the heavy weight of the iron head. He found he needed both hands to lift the heavy tool he'd seen Ezekiel wield with ease. Without thinking, Finn swung at the nearby log. The sharp blade dug into the wood with a satisfying *thud*. He wrenched the blade free, scattering wooden flakes over his shoulder, and swung it again.

He felt a little better. Chopping the wood with the heavy axe was oddly therapeutic. It offered a kind of release for the anger and fear welling up in his chest. Finn pulled the axe free from the log and whirled toward a nearby pine tree, sinking the head deep into the live wood. He pulled the blade free roughly, gouging out a piece of pine the size of his fist, and swung it at another tree, a tall, thin oak. The axe hit at an angle, causing the blade to slice off a long strip of bark.

Finn moved deeper into the woods, striking tree after tree with his grandfather's axe. Without noticing, he began to grunt and growl with each strike of the blade. He clenched his teeth and narrowed his eyes and let his anger at the injustice of it all wash over him. He squared his feet at the nearest tree—an immense oak with curtains of thick Spanish moss—reared back, and swung the axe as hard as he could.

A thin arm shot out of the trunk and caught the axe just before it bit into the wood. Finn froze in surprise, staring at the small hand that gripped the axe handle just below the iron head. When the hand jerked the axe free from Finn's grip, the surprising force disrupted his balance, and he fell backward onto the damp earth. He barely noticed falling; his gaze was fixed on the ghostly arm extending from the tree.

As he watched, the arm extended farther and farther until a pretty Asian woman in a sundress stepped out of the base of the tree. The axe looked impossibly heavy in her delicate arm, but she held it with the same ease she might hold a flower. Her jet-black hair almost reached her waist, and her skin gave off a pale, unearthly glow.

But her eyes startled Finn most. She had no pupils or irises; her eyes were solid green. When she glared down at Finn with disdain, he worried he might fall into the bottomless emerald pools.

"Why are you doing this?" she asked, reproaching him.

"I-I-I'm sorry!" Finn stammered. "I was just chopping wood, I didn't know—"

"You were not in need of wood for warmth, or to build!" the woman retorted. "You were letting rage consume you at the expense of the forest!"

"I was just... mad," Finn said. He looked down at his shoes and felt tremendously foolish.

"Your madness damaged half a dozen trees. Two of which will die, for nothing but your vanity."

"I wasn't trying to kill anything!"

"Trying has nothing to do with it," she snapped. "Your grandfather just spoke about responsibility. Do you not think it applies to the world around you?"

"How do you know what my grandfather said?" he asked.

"I am a Kodama. I know everything that happens in the forest."

"What's a Kodama?"

"Some people call us nymphs, or dryads. We are beings of the wood. My life force is tied to the nature surrounding us."

"So, you're like, a nature spirit?" Finn asked.

"I am a caretaker," the woman said. She stepped closer to Finn. "But so are you."

"What do you mean?"

"Your grandfather told you, that if you would wield a weapon, you have an obligation to do so not only with skill, but with concern and responsibility for those around you. The same is true of the *earth* around you. If you would use the ground, the wood, or the animals, you should learn to be a good steward."

"A steward?" he repeated.

"A person who looks after something they don't own. It's the duty of those who utilize the world to be good stewards, regardless of ownership."

Finn nodded. The anger that drove him through the woods vanished, but the sadness and sorrow felt more potent than ever. His gaze returned to the ground as he blinked back tears.

"I'm sorry I hit those trees. I was upset. But I shouldn't have done it."

Finn was surprised to feel a hand on his shoulder. He looked up into the face of the Kodama. Her solid-green eyes showed a concern in contrast with her previously stern tone.

She knelt down beside him, observing him closely. The axe lay in the grass nearby. Finn brushed the sleeve of his hoodie across his face and sniffled slightly.

"Why are you so upset?"

"I'm human. When I leave here at the end of the summer, I'm going to forget everything."

"Everything?" the Kodama asked.

"All the magical stuff, anyways. Probably even this." Finn gestured at himself and the Kodama.

"How?"

"The Auditor. He put a spell or something on this place, so humans can't remember any of the supernatural stuff when they leave."

"I'm familiar with the protections over this land, and with the being you call 'The Auditor.' Though both are immensely powerful, neither can truly take away your memory," she said softly.

"What do you mean?"

"The Auditor's protective veil keeps humans from recalling the otherworldly. But memory is more than recollection. When something impacts us, it becomes a part of who we are. You are already changed, Finn. You cannot change back. Just because you can't bring your experiences to your mind's eye, doesn't mean they didn't happen." The Kodama brushed Finn's hair from his eyes and offered a reassuring smile. "Memory is the shape left by the past, and that can never be taken away."

Finn wasn't sure he fully understood everything the Kodama said, but he felt a little better. He thanked her, and she offered him her hand.

Together, they walked out of the woods and back toward the house. Small but vibrant purple flowers sprouted along the sides of the trail as the Kodama moved along. A breeze swept through the flowers, and Finn caught hints of vanilla and cinnamon. He lost himself in the flowers' pleasing aroma, and he was eventually surprised to look up and see the Thin House in front of him.

Finn saw Ezekiel standing nearby. His grandfather's worried expression hit Finn like a semi-truck.

He took a deep breath and started to apologize for storming away, but his words were cut off by his grandfather wrapping him in a fierce hug.

Finn felt the last bit of anxiety and fear slip away, none of it any match for the warmth and safety that radiated from Ezekiel's embrace.

Eventually, Ezekiel leaned back and looked at Finn. "I know you're scared. But just because you forget something here—" Ezekiel tapped his head. "—doesn't mean you forget it here." He tapped Finn's chest.

Finn nodded and stared into his grandfather's piercing blue eyes.

"Nothing stored in the heart can ever be taken from you. I promise."

Finn believed him. He turned back to thank the Kodama for her advice, but she was gone. He could only make out the trail of purple flowers already fading into the forest.

He shrugged and left with Ezekiel to get lunch. Later, they helped Eleanor in the garden, and everything felt just right.

CHAPTER EIGHT: THE GHOST

One evening, as Finn and Eden played *Risk* with Mr. Gareth and Lahela in the library, the ghost in the attic began to wail. The group paused briefly in their game as the ghostly shriek echoed down through the house.

Over the past two months, the ghostly wails had largely become white noise, like a ceiling fan squeak or the hum of an air conditioner. When he first got to his grandparents' house, the noise was alarming—to say the least. The screams woke him on his second night, and his grandmother's calm explanation of, "Oh, don't worry, we just have a ghost in the attic," did little to soothe him. However, as Finn grew acclimated to the more supernatural aspects of the Thin House, a ghost in the attic seemed rather boring compared to some of the more exciting guests.

After a few moments, the haunting cacophony grew softer and softer, until it faded into a barely perceptible moan.

Eden turned to Mr. Gareth. "I'm attacking Kamchatka."

"A bold gambit, indeed," said Mr. Gareth, picking up the defense dice.

Finn stared up toward the attic.

His grandmother mentioned once that the ghost in the attic wasn't dangerous. According to Eleanor, the spirit suffered greatly during her life, and the cries were not to be feared but pitied. Finn and Eden tried to see the ghost once or twice, but she was never visible during the day.

The attic, however, was interesting enough on its own. In most homes, attics were spaces to store things that weren't worth displaying or using regularly but still contained enough value to keep. The Thin House was no exception—but the Thin House had a stranger and more eclectic history than other homes. Over the years, the supernatural boarding house accumulated an impressive amount of peculiar artifacts, souvenirs, and assorted otherworldly knick-knacks. The attic evolved into a chaotic museum dedicated to its unusual clientele.

The first time they ventured up the stairs to the attic, Finn and Eden were disappointed by the lack of ghosts, but they still spent hours searching through the bizarre assortment of Thin House history. They found ancient bronze chests that were impossibly large on the inside; small animal sculptures with jeweled eyes that changed colors; and several suitcases and duffel bags left behind by guests. After a short debate on the ethics of snooping in people's old luggage, Finn and Eden promptly opened every suitcase they could.

Though their search yielded mostly clothing, including a suit Finn assumed once belonged to a giant, they also found a jar containing a miniature city—complete with sky scrapers, a monorail, and a small green patch Finn identified as a park. When he looked closely, he was amazed at the detail in the tiny model. He thought he saw tiny cars driving down the roads.

Eden tried to open the jar, but the lid wouldn't budge. They decided to put it gently back into the suitcase and leave it be.

The only luggage the snooping pair failed to examine intensely was an old, leather briefcase. The briefcase was unremarkable, like most briefcases: slightly-faded, brown leather; peeling lettering on one side reading, "Peace of Mind Financial"; and a small, old-fashioned combination lock that barred it from further inspection by the curious children.

But in one of the corners, the children found a monogrammed message. Finn thought the gold threads would have looked rather nice before time faded the leather. Eden peered closely at the inscription and read it aloud.

"To James, with love."

They'd thought about busting the lock to examine the contents, but after reading the intimate inscription, it didn't feel right. Besides, Finn pointed out, it was likely just business papers. The two gave the attic one more cursory check for any ghosts before moving on to another activity.

But as Mr. Gareth, Eden, and Lahela tried to conquer the world in his grandparents' library, Finn wondered about the ghost in the attic. He wondered how a ghost ended up haunting the Thin House, of all places.

"Mr. Gareth, what do you know about the ghost?"

Mr. Gareth rolled the attack dice. "What ghost?" he asked, without even looking up.

Finn blinked at Mr. Gareth as another moan echoed from the attic.

The old vampire raised his eyebrows in recognition. "Ah, you mean Ms. Abigail?"

"Ms. Abigail?" Eden asked, interested, despite her aggressive colonization of Asia.

"Was that her name?" Finn asked.

"Still is, I suppose," Mr. Gareth mused.

"Did you know her?" Lahela asked. She sat on a pillow next to Eden. Finn thought she seemed particularly cheerful lately—not at all skittish like she had been when they first met. She'd been spending a lot of time with the old vampire. Mr. Gareth told her long, overly-detailed stories, and Lahela seemed to enjoy them.

"Not personally, no. But I'm familiar with her story."

Finn waited, but the normally verbose vampire didn't continue. "Who was she?"

"It's not really a story for children."

"Maybe not regular children, but I can turn into a wolf, and he's been living with monsters all summer," Eden retorted.

"A fair point indeed, young lady," Mr. Gareth agreed. "Nevertheless, your mother and grandparents would not appreciate my sharing this particular tale." He glanced at Lahela questioningly.

"Please? We won't get scared or anything," Finn pleaded.

Mr. Gareth scratched his chin. Finn could see him torn between his desire to share information and his responsibility as an adult not to alarm children. He looked at Lahela again, who shrugged. Eventually, the vampire's love of stories won out.

"Very well, but I did warn you. This does not have a happy ending."

Mr. Gareth watched to see if that would deter the children—he sighed when it did not.

"Ms. Abigail was the first guest at the Thin House."

"What was she?" Eden asked.

"She was a human. She wandered across the bridge on the very first night Ezekiel and Eleanor opened the boarding house. She was in a rather frightful state, and your grandparents tried to offer their assistance."

"Frightful state?" Finn repeated.

"She was shaking and sobbing uncontrollably. She was covered in dirt, as if she had been walking for a long time. She didn't seem physically hurt at all, but whenever your grandparents tried to comfort her, she moaned and cried even harder. They thought about calling for help, but the protections on the property complicate things. Instead, they decided to make her comfortable for the night and take her to town for help in the morning."

"So what happened?"

"Eleanor cleaned her up, and they settled her in the attic. It used to be a rather cozy room. They gave her some food and promised her they would help however they could in the morning. Ms. Abigail was still crying, but she was calmer. They left her in relative comfort. But when they checked on her in the morning... She had taken her own life."

Eden gasped, and Finn sighed sadly.

Mr. Gareth continued.

"Your grandparents tried to contact her next-of-kin, but she'd only given them a first name. She had no other papers or letters to identify her. Eleanor and Ezekiel spent days searching, but they were unable to find any family. They buried her at the cemetery in town. The night of the funeral, her spirit returned. Ezekiel discovered her sitting in the attic, crying by the window."

"Poor thing," Lahela said sadly.

"Has anyone tried to talk to her?" Finn asked.

"Oh yes. Eleanor and Ezekiel have tried to communicate with her many times over the years. I even tried once myself. But she never reacts."

"I don't understand, though, everybody dies. How come she became a ghost? You said she was a human, did dying here make her a ghost?" Finn asked.

"Yes and no," said Mr. Gareth, adjusting his glasses. "This world is full of spirits who have concerns that tie them to this plane after their life is finished. However, the veil that is lifted here is quite thick over the rest of the earth. Most spirits are unable to interact with us at all. Ms. Abigail is not a ghost *because* she died here—but we can perceive her because of the nature of this property."

"So ghosts can't move on if their concerns aren't resolved?" Eden asked.

"That is the theory. Though, I did know a delightful phantom in Budapest who claims he accidentally slept through his own death. Not that he minds! In fact—"

Finn interrupted before Mr. Gareth could derail their conversation. "So for Ms. Abigail to move on, we need to figure out what she's holding on to, and help her find closure?"

Mr. Gareth considered the question for a moment. He seemed slightly uncomfortable when he replied. "Theoretically, yes. But, Finn, grief is a complicated emotion. You have to be careful you don't make things worse."

"There can't be much worse than being stuck as a crying shadow in an attic forever," Finn reasoned. "Would the library have old newspapers?"

"Yes," Mr. Gareth sighed, picking up the pieces of the game that would go unfinished. "There are binders with the local paper going back to 1869 near the biographies. Your grandparents opened the boarding home in 1873."

"Thanks, Mr. Gareth!"

Finn and Eden hopped up and hurried to the biographies. As they left the table, Mr. Gareth turned to Lahela and sighed, "Four hundred years, and I cannot finish a game of *Risk*."

⌂

Finn and Eden searched all the newspapers published in 1873. The local paper ran daily, so there was a lot to sift through. Finn read about baby and wedding announcements from local, often-wealthy citizens; businesses opening and closing; and the occasional traveling fair. Eden discovered a story about a local goat that could do somersaults. However, they read through mostly mundane articles for hours before they found anything.

"This is interesting," Eden said, passing an article to Finn. "October 5, 1873."

He looked down at the bold headline reading, "Paper Mill Fire Rages On."

Eden bent over Finn's shoulder, summarizing the story. "It caught fire during lunch, but it was too powerful for the locals to get close. They kept it from spreading, but the building was still burning when they published the article."

"I read an article from when the mill opened that said they were hiring over a hundred people. A lot of workers were probably inside."

"Let's check the next one," Eden suggested.

Finn flipped through the binder until they got to the paper from October 6, 1873. Finn pulled it from its sleeve in the binder and held it where both he and Eden could see it clearly. The front page featured the burnt, skeletal frame of a massive building. The headline read, "Three Dead at Mill Fire."

"Just Three? That factory had over a hundred employees. Did the rest just walk out?" Finn wondered.

"No," Eden said, skimming through the article. "It says the owners had sponsored an employee lunch at the Elks Lodge, and the building was almost empty when the fire started."

"Almost empty? So who was there?" Finn asked.

"The two owners didn't attend the lunch. Their... remains were found trapped in an office. It says the only staff member not accounted for is a secretary... Abigail Peters."

"Ms. Abigail? But she couldn't have been the third person. She died here, not at the fire."

Eden kept reading. As Finn watched, he saw her eyes widen in surprise and then soften with sadness. She looked up solemnly at Finn.

"It wasn't her. It says the third body was too small... Most likely a child."

"A child..." Finn said softly.

⌂

As far as Finn could tell, the weather at his grand-parents' seemed frozen in a perpetual state of late fall. When he first arrived in May, Finn was surprised by the autumn breeze that masked the summer air. Since that day, the weather had not warmed or cooled, merely persisted. When he asked his grandmother about it, she was busy snatching up a chocolate bar before Chester could get to it.

Distracted, she muttered, "That's what we get for opening on Halloween."

So, over the course of the next two months, Finn became accustomed to cool days and colder nights warmed by the ever-burning fireplace.

The attic was different. Stepping over the threshold into the dark, cluttered attic reminded Finn of entering the deep freeze at his mother's restaurant. The first time Eden and Finn explored the attic, he ended up putting on a black fur coat they found. The coat had a bear's head for a hood, and it kept Finn quite toasty.

As he stepped into the strangely-chilled room again, Finn zipped up his red hoodie and pulled the hood over his head.

Finn was alone as he walked through the cluttered artifacts of bygone visitors. Eden decided to tag along on a late-night run with her mother for the full moon.

He scanned the room cautiously as he wove around a pile of suitcases. He didn't know what to expect, exactly. A plethora of horror movies and ghost stories had him looking for a wispy, shimmering figure made of silver smoke. However, Finn spent most of the summer being surprised at how dissimilar the Thin House guests were from their Halloween counterparts. He tried to stay alert and keep an open mind.

"Ms. Abigail? Are you here?"

A soft but sudden noise made Finn jump. His heart raced, but he listened closely and could hear someone sobbing. He tried to move toward the noise, but he couldn't pinpoint the source of the weeping. He stopped moving and listened carefully. He breathed deeply and slowly, steaming the cold air around him. He focused and, thinking of the Lagahoo, tried to "see" like Ezekiel had taught him.

The attic was still empty.

Finn sighed. He glanced around one last time and turned back toward the stairs. He could still hear the soft sobbing, but there was no sign of the ghostly Ms. Abigail.

Then, icy fingers glided across the back of his neck. He bit down a scream as he whirled in the direction of the spectral touch.

A middle-aged black woman in a simple but old-fashioned dress stood by the circular window overlooking the front yard. She stared through the glass as frosty tears cracked down her cheeks. She wasn't translucent, like Finn thought she would be. She looked indistinguishable from a living person, with one exception—she cast no shadow in the moonlight that spilled through the window.

"Ms. Abigail?"

The ghost did not acknowledge him. Her sobs grew a touch louder, but she continued to stare out the window. He stepped toward her, and the room grew colder the closer he moved. As he approached Ms. Abigail, he saw soot on her hands and wrists.

Ice crystals crunched under his sneakers as he came to a stop.

"Ms. Abigail, I know what happened... to your daughter."

Ms. Abigail's shoulders had been shaking, but she froze at Finn's words. She made no move to turn, but her sudden stillness emboldened him. He took a breath and continued.

"It's okay, Ms. Abigail. It wasn't your fault. You were just trying to provide for your little girl. I guess they let her stay with you at the office? You couldn't have known there was going to be a fire."

Everything flashed, and Ms. Abigail was suddenly nose-to-nose with Finn, glaring furiously at him. Her dark, angry eyes held Finn. Though she wasn't touching him, she sent icy tendrils spiraling toward him, piercing the thin fabric of his hoodie. Involuntary shivers racked his frame. He tried to step back, but the ghost's fearsome attention kept him frozen in place.

Ms. Abigail clenched her jaw, and her lips peeled back, revealing teeth that shone like pearls. Finn thought for one horrifying moment that she would bite him.

She began to cry.

She did not cry soft sobs like before, but piercing wails that filled the air. She bent over, steadying herself on her knees as she moaned and wept. Icy tears fell steadily onto the wooden floor of the attic.

Finn considered running, but he stopped and thought about the ghostly woman before him. He thought about her alone up there, forever mourning the daughter who'd passed on long before her.

Finn knew he had to try again.

"Ms. Abigail... I'm so sorry. But she's been gone for a long time. Wherever she is, I'm sure she's at peace. You should be, too."

Ms. Abigail threw her head back and screamed.

Finn, who'd spent months listening to wailing and moaning as it echoed from the attic, was completely unprepared for the sudden, thunderous shriek. He covered his ears in a vain attempt to block out the piercing cries, but his hands did nothing to block out the all-consuming scream. He fell to his knees.

He was dimly aware of Ms. Abigail gliding away from him toward the window. He forced himself to look up.

She leaned sorrowfully against the glass, still screaming. She banged her fist against the window, and the entire attic shook.

Finn averted his gaze and began to crawl away. He eventually pulled himself toward the doorway. Still covering his ears, he inch-wormed his way over the threshold, hooked his foot around the door, and pulled it shut. Then, he managed to get to his feet and hobble to his bedroom.

The noise wasn't quite as maddening downstairs, but Finn spent the rest of the night in bed with a pillow over his head. He did his best to block out Ms. Abigail's miserable cries, but he didn't sleep.

Around sunrise, the wails finally softened before gradually stopping altogether. Finn stumbled out of bed and groggily lurched downstairs for breakfast.

When Finn entered the kitchen, Eleanor was pulling bacon out of a frying pan with a pair of tongs. Chester was passed out on a chair, snoring lightly. Finn slid in across from the tired jackalope and held his head while his grandmother stacked his plate full of food.

Chester's eyes opened, and he shuffled sleepily to the edge of the chair. The jackalope leaned against the table with his front paws and looked at Finn pleadingly.

Finn gave Chester half a pancake and looked at his grandmother. The normally bright and chipper woman was yawning every minute or so and seemed to have trouble focusing on cooking the eggs.

"I'm guessing your experiment didn't go well?" she asked, a little ironically.

Finn yawned. "In the movies, a ghost sticks around because they have unfinished business. I thought if she knew that her daughter had moved on, maybe she would, too."

"She had a daughter?"

"We found an article about Ms. Abigail. She was the only survivor of a fire that killed a child. The two other bodies were the owners, and they were both bachelors."

"Yes, the Beldam Brothers, I remember them," Eleanor offered.

"Well, you know how the paper always prints announcements for all the new babies born?"

"Yes."

"We found one for Jacquelyn Peters, born to Abigail Peters. A few years before the fire."

"You think she brought her daughter to work?"

"Yes, and somehow they got separated and… The girl didn't make it."

"Seems like a decent theory," Eleanor agreed.

"So why didn't it work?" Finn asked, crunching into a thick piece of bacon.

"Work?"

"Yeah, why couldn't I fix it?"

Eleanor turned to him and shook her head softly. "You don't fix grief, Finn."

"But I thought—"

Eleanor held up a hand. "Finn, I have a daughter that I barely hear from. She hasn't visited in years, and she gets anxious talking to me. I am still learning to live with that pain. I can't imagine losing a daughter the way you are describing. I don't believe it's something that can be wrapped up tidily with a few hours of research and a nice talk. Besides, there's no telling what else happened between the fire and her showing up here."

"What do you mean?" Finn asked.

"I never thought of connecting Ms. Abigail to the fire, because it happened several weeks before she showed up."

"The fire happened on the fifth of October," Finn said.

"That's right. But we opened on Halloween."

"So she spent weeks wandering like that?"

"Maybe. Or maybe something else happened. My point is, that we don't know the whole story, and it's hard to fully understand someone else's tragedy."

"So that's it, then? There's nothing I can do to help?" Finn asked sadly.

Eleanor smiled and placed a reassuring hand on his shoulder. "We can always help people in need. I'm just saying that grief is a long and complicated journey. Sometimes, all we can do is make sure the grieving don't go through the worst of it alone. Sometimes, we just have to mourn *with* those that mourn."

⌂

That night, Finn ventured into the attic again. He waited in the growing cold until Ms. Abigail appeared in her usual place beside the window. She was sobbing, as usual, but in the manner the Thin House knew best, not the piercing, heartbroken shrieks of the previous evening. Ms. Abigail kept her back to Finn, making no move to acknowledge him.

Finn watched her for a moment, steadying himself. Then, he took a tentative step toward the sobbing apparition. Ice crunched under his sneakers as he closed the gap between her and himself.

When Finn was mere inches from the weeping ghost, he paused. He closed his eyes for a moment, took a breath, and let himself feel the waves of loss cascading off the ghostly mother. Ms. Abigail still paid Finn no attention and continued to moan softly, all the while gazing listlessly out the window.

"Ms. Abigail... I'm sorry."

Finn reached over and put an arm around the grieving mother. Ms. Abigail flinched at his touch, paused momentarily, and then leaned her face into his shoulder. She let out a soft moan and continued crying softly. Her tears soaked through the fabric of his sweatshirt. He was surprised to find that the chill had vanished, and Ms. Abigail felt warm against him. He patted her arm comfortingly.

Her sobs changed, though he couldn't articulate the difference. She cried as if releasing a great burden.

Or perhaps just sharing it.

No moans emanated from the attic that night. Many of the Thin House regulars slept poorly in the strange, peaceful silence that fell over the house. Finn stayed with Ms. Abigail, occasionally whispering comforting words, sometimes asking casual questions about Jacquelyn, but mostly just sitting. Ms. Abigail cried a lot of soft, gentle tears that seemed to offer genuine relief.

Eventually, she told Finn all about her daughter: how much she loved biscuits and tomato gravy, how good she was at counting, how much she enjoyed the stories Ms. Abigail told her at bedtime. Finn gradually fell asleep to her stories.

When he woke the next morning, he was laying on the floor of the attic by the window. Sunlight streamed into the room, and Finn was wrapped in a blanket he didn't remember seeing the previous night. He folded the blanket neatly and started downstairs.

Ms. Abigail would most likely be crying again some night soon. But she wouldn't always be alone.

Not if he could help it.

CHAPTER NINE: THE MONSTER

The monster escaped on a Sunday like any other Sunday. Ezekiel and Eleanor went to church. Lahela went shopping in town. None of the other guests stirred.

Finn, Eden, and Chester watched cartoons. The trio munched on popcorn despite Eleanor telling them not to snack too much. She'd planned a big Sunday dinner because the following week, Lahela and Eden would be moving out. They'd leave two days before Finn went home. Considering even casual, Tuesday-night dinners at the Thin House were like feasts, Finn wondered where they would possibly fit the food for what he knew would be the largest meal he'd seen in his life.

Despite the idyllic Sunday morning and the promise of a spectacular dinner, Finn felt badly. His mother reminded him the previous night that she would pick him up on Thursday. Finn was not looking forward to saying goodbye to Eden, to Mr. Gareth, or to his grandparents. And he couldn't stop worrying about the impending loss of his memories. He wondered if the memories would go gradually, or if he'd forget all at once—if he'd step over the bridge and have no memory of Chester, Ms. Abigail, or his other new friends. He tried to focus on the present and enjoy the time he had, but something else kept bothering Finn: his nightmare.

Ms. Abigail had been relatively quiet, so Finn slept in his room. He'd gone to bed feeling fine, but the dream that unfolded made him worry that he'd been running a high fever.

It started with Finn wandering in a dark network of underground tunnels. It was almost pitch-black, and he could barely see where he was going. As he wandered, he noticed framed pictures nailed into the stony walls of the caves. Each frame gave off a slight glow, illuminating its contents. But whenever he examined the pictures, the contents blurred.

He didn't spend much time examining the pictures, because he wasn't alone. As he walked, he heard something following him, something big. It sounded like cockroaches scrambling on dried cardboard—spiderlike, with sharp, rapid steps that sped up whenever he stopped walking.

Finn started to run.

As he hurried through the shadowy labyrinth, Finn heard the monstrous thing gaining on him. He thought he heard it laughing. But then, Finn realized the short, harsh laughter was really panting, eager breath— the anticipation of a predator about to feed. Finn felt panic rise in his throat, and a scream tried to force its way through his clenched teeth. He rounded a corner and found himself in a circular room with no other tunnels attached. He started back the way he'd come, but he could hear the monstrous thing approaching. Out of options, he ran into the circular room and looked for something, *anything* that could help.

On the opposite wall, Finn saw a frame almost as tall as him. He walked closer and found a full length mirror instead of a photograph. Finn stepped into view and gasped.

Reflected in the mirror, he saw the rumpled suit, greasy hair, and sharp eyes that he'd last seen staring up at him from the well in the basement. The grin was gone. The reflection in the mirror panted and looked utterly terrified. But Finn was staring at the unmistakable visage of the Rictus.

Finn raised a sweaty hand and moved it back and forth in disbelief. The haggard man in the mirror mimicked the motion perfectly. Finn shook his head, not comprehending — then froze in horror.

Through the mirror, he watched the approach of a shape so black, it left a void in the darkness of the cavern. The shape wasn't human. It was too big, too asymmetrical, and too... alien. Finn felt its hot breath on the back of his neck and felt its jagged, gaping maw unhinge. The horrible mouth of the monster leaned down to consume him, and Finn screamed.

He shot up in his bed, exploding out of sleep with a suddenness that rattled his chest. Even as he sat enjoying cartoons on a bright, Sunday morning, Finn cringed at the thought of that spiderlike skittering following him into the darkness.

Eden watched him expectantly, and Finn realized she'd asked him a question. He'd completely missed it.

"What did you say?" he asked.

"I asked if you think that's weird." Eden pointed toward the hallway.

Finn followed her finger and saw Chester. The jackalope stood near the hallway entrance, staring at the grandfather clock. Finn watched curiously as the normally twitchy animal stood stock still, staring at the clock as if preparing to bolt in terror. Finn stood up and walked toward the hallway.

"You don't think there's something… wrong down there?" he asked Eden.

"Aren't there alarms and stuff? If it gets loose, I mean."

"My grandfather said the alarms go off if it crosses the threshold. But it could have gotten loose and just be waiting in the basement."

"Should we call your grandparents?"

"I don't know. All we really have to go on is that Chester's freaked out."

"Chester was freaked out last time," Eden countered.

"Still…" Finn said, uncertain.

Chester stared anxiously at the hidden basement door. Finn thought of his dream and their last encounter with the Rictus. He felt for the obsidian knife, and when he found it stuffed in the back pocket of his jeans, he was a little reassured.

He turned back to Eden.

"Let's just peek in. We'll stay on the stairs and just look, to make sure it's still locked up. If there's anything wrong with the lock, we turn around and call my grandparents."

Eden nodded, and they walked toward the clock.

As Finn turned the hands of the timepiece to activate the doorway, Chester spooked. He ran past the children and up the stairs to the guest rooms. Finn tried not to read into the jackalope's terror. He heard the lock click open, and he rolled the clock aside to reveal the door.

Eden placed a hand on his shoulder. Finn was surprised to see that his usually-fearless friend seemed hesitant.

"We just check to see if it's still locked up, right?" she asked.

Finn nodded and opened the door. The sudden gust of chilled air hit both children as they crossed the threshold and descended the steps. Finn led the way down until they finally reached a point where they could see the room clearly.

Finn breathed a sigh of relief when he saw that the heavy grate covering the well was shut.

He turned to Eden, but something caught his attention. He narrowed his eyes and scanned the side of the well.

The latch was empty—no sign of the lock.

Finn scanned the room again and noticed that one of the glowing stones was missing. One corner of the room was shrouded in darkness.

Both children stared in horror at the patch of darkness and flinched as something flew out of the shadows. It skidded to the foot of the stairs before clattering to a stop.

The iron lock.

Finn and Eden whirled around to dart up the stairs. But Finn felt something grab the collar of his sweatshirt, and he was suddenly yanked backward.

"Ah ah ah, not so fast, children," laughed a cold voice mirthlessly from the darkness.

Finn rolled over in time to see the Rictus step out of the shadows. A jagged tendril made of black oil slid out the sleeve of his suit as he grinned at Finn and Eden.

"We haven't had a chance to visit yet," the Rictus said, feigning sadness through gritted teeth.

Finn heard a growl and the sound of fabric ripping. When he looked back, Eden was gone. A large wolf with auburn fur stood in her place. The wolf flashed large, razor-sharp teeth, then launched itself at the pale, grinning man who stood over Finn. She released a fierce, guttural roar—which was cut off suddenly, as the Rictus sprang forward with unearthly quickness.

The thin figure vaulted over Finn and caught the leaping wolf by the neck. Pale fingers dug into the flesh of her throat. Eden choked and strained against the impossible grip of the monster, and the Rictus shook her violently in the air.

Finn pulled the knife from his back pocket, sprawled forward, and plunged the blade into the back of the Rictus's leg.

The Rictus barely flinched. He reached down absent-mindedly and slapped Finn so hard, the boy almost passed out.

Finn managed to hang onto the knife, but the force of the blow sent him rolling to the side.

When he tried to get up, the Rictus brandished a finger in warning. The monster held the wolf by the throat with one hand and made a finger gun with the other. Finn watched in horror as the Rictus's finger peeled back, and a jagged, black spike emerged from underneath the skin. The tip of the protrusion looked sharp, like the fang of a snake. The spike grew until the barb was millimeters away from Eden's eye.

The Rictus grinned at Finn.

"As much as I enjoy hurting you, boy, it's time for me to leave this prison." The pale man nodded toward the door at the top of the stairs. "Open the door."

Finn looked at the stairway. "You need me to open it. You need a human," he said.

"If you want your friend to survive, you'll do it quickly," the Rictus leered.

"That is quite enough!"

The Rictus and Finn both turned toward the voice.

Mr. Gareth stood resolutely on the stairs, wearing his house slippers and a thick red cardigan Eleanor knitted a couple weeks back. His hair was slightly disheveled, and his bowtie was askew, but the vampire-librarian had a stern expression on his face, and he pointed authoritatively at the Rictus.

"Release the young lady immediately!" Mr. Gareth ordered.

The Rictus met Mr. Gareth's gaze. He didn't release Eden, but he tilted his head curiously at the vampire as if pleasantly surprised.

"This doesn't concern you. You should leave while I still allow it."

"I will tolerate no violence against these children." He narrowed his eyes behind his round spectacles. "You will release them and return to your cell, or I shall be forced to take aggressive action."

"You're more suited for gathering dust than making threats. You won't save them... Just like you didn't save her." The grinning man winked at the vampire.

Something flashed across Mr. Gareth's face for an instant, but he quickly composed himself. Instead, the vampire smiled and nodded softly.

He removed his glasses and slid them into the inner pocket of his shirt.

"In his purest form, the librarian is a guide to knowledge." Mr. Gareth pushed up the sleeves of his cardigan. "It is the librarian's duty to lead others to wisdom, like Virgil leading Dante through the underworld."

The Rictus rolled his eyes. "How does this concern me?"

"Because while I consider it my calling to impart wisdom—" Mr. Gareth's lips peeled back, revealing an imposing pair of fangs. "—the unfortunate truth is, some people only learn one way."

There was a blur of red, and suddenly, Eden fell to the floor along with the Rictus's left hand. Mr. Gareth stood between the Rictus and the fallen wolf. His hand was raised, and thick, black blood dripped from fingernails that grew into razor-sharp claws.

Mr. Gareth turned his head toward Finn.

"Get out of here, now!" the vampire roared.

Finn hurried to Eden's side. She was breathing, but she made no move to rise to her feet.

Behind him, he heard the Rictus burst into harsh laughter. He glanced over his shoulder and saw three tendrils unfurl from the black mass dripping out of his wounded wrist.

Mr. Gareth seized the Rictus by his greasy hair. As Finn watched, Mr. Gareth wrenched the Rictus's head to one side and plunged his fangs into the pale man's neck.

Finn turned back to Eden. Though he couldn't see any visible injuries, she wasn't moving. He took a breath and scooped his arms under her heavy frame, shifting her weight and lifting with his legs. Ezekiel once showed him how to do a fireman's carry. At the time, Finn never thought he would need to use it on an unconscious werewolf.

Behind him, he heard Mr. Gareth gag and splutter. He craned his head and saw the vampire hacking up the Rictus's oil-like blood.

The Rictus sighed.

The gash on his neck knitted back together with black fluid.

Then, he rammed three sharp tendrils into Mr. Gareth's ribs. The vine-like shoots dug into his flesh.

Mr. Gareth sliced at the tendrils with his razor-sharp nails. The black growths severed from the Rictus, but as Finn watched, new ones began to sprout.

Finn adjusted the wolf's weight and started up the stairs. After just a few steps, he felt himself tiring. He could hear Mr. Gareth groaning behind him and felt guilty for not being able to help. Finn strained against his friend's weight and forced his way farther up the stairs.

He heard a particularly painful groan and turned in time to see the Rictus wrap four tendrils from his severed hand around Mr. Gareth's throat. The monster slammed the vampire hard against the stone wall of the basement.

Mr. Gareth's form slumped.

The Rictus dragged the librarian back then hoisted him into the air. Mr. Gareth dangled several feet off the ground, straining with both hands against the tendrils as they slowly forced the air from his lungs.

The Rictus shook his head contemptuously.

"You thought you could challenge me, vampire? I was old when your species first crawled out of the shadows."

Mr. Gareth gargled something unintelligible. The Rictus furrowed its brow and lowered Mr. Gareth slightly. The tendrils around the vampire's neck loosened.

"What was that? A final thought?"

Mr. Gareth sucked in some air, cleared his throat, and grinned with blood in his teeth.

"I called for help before coming down."

Finn heard a rush of air as the basement door opened. Something large rushed past him and Eden, and several gunshots echoed down in the basement. Eleanor stood at the top of the stairs holding a hunting rifle. At the bottom, Ezekiel charged toward the Rictus, firing several shots from his Colt in quick succession.

Both his grandparents wore their church clothes.

Ezekiel had managed to ditch his tie and suitcoat, but he'd strapped his weapons belt over his dress pants and shirt. And Finn couldn't help thinking how strange his grandmother looked, holding the rifle in her floral-print Sunday dress.

The forty-five caliber slugs sent the Rictus stumbling back into the dark corner of the room.

Mr. Gareth fell to the floor, but Ezekiel helped the vampire to his feet. Eleanor hurried toward Finn. She helped him shoulder some of the wolf's weight and started guiding them both up the stairs.

Finn looked back toward his grandfather.

Ezekiel and Mr. Gareth stood facing the dark patch of the basement. Ezekiel had his gun raised, and the vampire-librarian spread his clawed hands.

The darkness expanded, and the Rictus burst back into the pale light. Six massive black tendrils emerged from the monster's back and formed into spider legs, raising the Rictus's human form high into the air. As Finn watched, the Rictus shot jagged, spear-like tendrils at Ezekiel and Mr. Gareth from his intact arm and severed wrist.

Both men rolled to avoid the onslaught. Ezekiel fired three quick shots. Black, oily matter exploded from the monster's pale flesh, but the wounds repaired as soon as they appeared. Ezekiel pressed on the release and flicked out the empty magazine, simultaneously pulling a replacement from his gun belt and loading it into the weapon.

"Finn!"

Eleanor's scream called Finn back to the matter at hand. Together, he and his grandmother carried the still-unconscious wolf up the stairs and through the basement door.

Chester hopped up the stairs behind them. They laid the wolf's prone form on the couch in the living room, and Finn started back toward the basement. His grandmother grabbed his shoulder.

"Where are you going?"

"We have to help them, right?" Finn asked, panting slightly.

"No " Eleanor shook her head. "If you go down there, you'll just give that monster something to use against your grandfather and Mr. Gareth. We need to stay here with— Oh no."

Finn followed her gaze to the window and saw a black car pulling up in the driveway. It took Finn a moment to recognize the Auditor's car.

Eleanor slid her rifle under the couch and began straightening her hair as she marched to the front door. "We have to stall him. If he has to intervene, we'll lose the house!"

Finn didn't move. Hearing his grandmother use the word "monster" reminded Finn of something his grandparents told him his first night in the house. A flood of memories from his time with his grandparents rushed through his mind, and suddenly, he had an idea.

He whirled around and ran toward the hallway.

Eleanor caught his shoulder. "Wait, where are you going?"

"I think I know how to stop it," he said, trying to shrug off his grandmother's arm.

"Finn, you can't go back—" Eleanor started, but he turned and looked her square in the eyes.

"You have to trust me. Try to stall the Auditor. I can do this."

Eleanor stared wordlessly at Finn for the briefest of moments, then marched toward the gun cabinet. As he watched, his grandmother produced a small golden key from a chain around her neck. She unlocked the cabinet doors and pulled out a large wooden box. When she lifted the lid, Finn was surprised to see a bar of dark baking chocolate. As soon as the chocolate was in sight, Chester's ears stood up, and the jackalope's eyes narrowed in sharp focus.

"What are you doing?" Finn asked.

Eleanor unwrapped the bar. "Buying us some time."

She broke off a hunk of the chocolate bar and tossed it to Chester. The jackalope pounced on the chocolatey morsel and gobbled it down.

"I thought he wasn't supposed to —"

Finn stopped abruptly when Chester shook with a violent spasm. The jackalope made a strange hissing noise, and as Finn watched, the creature grew. Before Finn could ask what was going on, Chester had grown to the size of a St. Bernard. His spine sprouted from his back and formed into armored ridges between his lean, muscular shoulders and tail. Six-inch-long talons emerged from each foot, and a ferocious-looking set of canines protruded from his lips.

Chester's antlers grew and twisted together until they were thicker than bulls' horns.

Finn stared open-mouthed. Eleanor snapped her fingers and pointed toward the hallway.

Chester bounded past Finn and hopped through the door leading to the basement.

Eleanor set the remainder of the chocolate back in the cabinet and began walking toward the front door. "I'll try to stall him. If you think you can do something, do it quickly. But be careful."

Finn ran down the hallway. He hurried past the door leading to the basement, ignoring the violent sounds emanating from below, and rushed up the main stairs. He took the steps two at a time, ignoring the ache in his legs and the shortness of his breath. When he reached the attic and crossed the threshold, the unearthly cold felt refreshing.

He tore through the clutter of the attic, desperately searching for the one thing he knew could save everyone. But he couldn't find it. Amidst the suitcases, clothes, and bizarre knick-knacks, he couldn't locate the object of his search. Finn pushed aside piles of clothes and towering stacks of luggage to no avail. Exhaustion started to overwhelm him, and he sank to one knee. Sweat rolled off him despite the cold while he tried to catch his breath.

"Come on. Gotta keep going," he muttered to himself.

Then something cold and ghostly brushed across the left side of his face. He turned and saw a strange breeze catch a newspaper on the other side of the room. As the paper fluttered, it revealed a corner of a leather briefcase.

"Yes!" Finn rushed toward the pile of debris and pulled the briefcase from it. He glanced at the familiar inscription and pulled his knife out of his back pocket.

"Sorry, James," Finn said. Then, he stabbed at the leather around the combination lock with the stone knife. The jagged edge cut through the leather like butter. He sawed away until the lock and the catch had been completely removed.

The contents appeared to be mostly clerical: papers, manila folders, a few dried-up pens. At first, he didn't see what he wanted. He shuffled through insurance form after insurance form before he finally saw a photograph at the bottom of the briefcase under all the complicated documents. He snatched up the small square and started for the door.

Then he paused for a moment at the threshold. Turning back to the seemingly empty attic, he said, "Thanks, Ms. Abigail." Then, he hurried back down the stairs.

Before entering the hidden basement door, Finn peeked into the living room. He saw Eden passed out under a heavy blanket, but there was no sign of the Auditor or his grandmother. Glancing through the nearest window, he saw them talking by his car. The strange man saw him looking—Finn thought his eyes narrowed slightly.

But Finn turned and hurried into the basement.

He returned to a scene of utter chaos. The Rictus's still-grinning human form dangled from a massive network of black spider legs that stretched almost to the ceiling. Barbed tentacles protruded like large worms from the man's body and viciously lashed out at Ezekiel, Mr. Gareth, and the transformed Chester. Ezekiel had drawn his Comanche knife and parried tentacles while shooting at the monster with his gun hand.

Chester tried to gore the Rictus with his massive horns and bit at the arachnoid legs with his curved, predatory teeth. The Rictus tried to latch onto Chester with his barbed tentacles, but the jackalope kept twitching out of the way at the last moment.

Mr. Gareth fought alongside the jackalope, but Finn could tell he was struggling. The vampire's cardigan was torn, and one of his arms hung limply at his side, covered in dark liquid—the creature's blood. As Finn watched, the black plasma burned Mr. Gareth's arm like slow-acting acid.

"Get out of here!" Ezekiel roared.

The Rictus's pale face rolled toward Finn. His eyes were unfocused, like the gaze of a dead fish, but his grin widened, somehow.

Suddenly, the man's head rolled back, and the paralytic grin shot open, and a whirling mass of clawing black tendrils emerged like rabid animals springing from a trap. The tendrils spiked and speared toward Finn.

Chester bolted forward and knocked him out of the way, taking the brunt of the attack. The barrage of tentacles hit him like a battering ram. There was an audible *thud*, and the giant-sized jackalope was sent hurtling into the stone wall of the basement.

As Chester slid down the cracked stone, Finn watched him slowly shrink back to his regular form before passing out.

Finn stumbled to his feet and stepped toward the towering mass of the Rictus. He reached into his pocket for the item from the briefcase, but Mr. Gareth rushed toward him, trying to whisk him to safety.

"Wait!" Finn held up a hand, but one of the Rictus's spider legs shot forward. Finn gasped as the monster's massive arachnoid leg pierced through Mr. Gareth's back and the front of his chest.

"No!" he screamed.

The vampire-librarian winced dully and fell to the floor as the Rictus pulled its leg free.

The monster turned back toward Finn just as Ezekiel leapt into the air, grabbing the Rictus by his human neck. Finn's grandfather forced the monster into a one-armed choke hold and raised his knife.

Finn rushed to Mr. Gareth's side. The vampire was still breathing, but his eyes were closed, and he wasn't moving. Finn slid off his jacket and wrapped it around the wound. He cinched it tight, while Ezekiel plunged his knife repeatedly into the pale man's side.

When the Comanche blade drove into the monster, Finn heard the flesh sizzle and burn. The creature winced and staggered.

Ezekiel didn't let up. The muscles in his bicep strained as he choked the pale man harder. His other hand was a whir of motion as he drove the Comanche blade between his opponent's ribs. The insectoid legs suspending the Rictus's human form lurched, lowering the pale man in the suit to the floor. Ezekiel landed on his feet, but the spider legs and tentacles dissolved.

Finn watched as all the black, oily matter congealed together into a single mass and collided with Ezekiel. His grandfather held fast, but the black liquid worked its way around his body until everything below his chest was consumed.

Ezekiel tried to push his way free, but the plasma worked up his arm and tightened around his wrist, sending his knife tumbling to the floor. The pale man slowly turned and glanced at Ezekiel, who was covered up to his neck in sludge. The veins in his neck and forehead popped as he struggled against the constricting, black mass.

"I tire of this dance, Ezekiel Blacklock. It is time for me to move on to more suitable partners."

"Stop!" Finn yelled.

"Get back, Finn!" Ezekiel roared. He tried to yell something else, but the black oil climbed higher and silenced him.

"You should have run while you could," the Rictus hissed at Finn.

"I'm going to stop you," Finn said, sounding more confident than he felt.

The next voice echoed inside Finn's skull, and he felt the words clawing their way through his soul. The voice was deep, ancient, and cold.

"I am the Fear that paralyzes, that halts armies and cripples heroes! I am the last feeling you shall ever know!"

The pale man's skin shuddered, and several pores expanded into small, dark holes. Finn heard a sharp hiss, and suddenly a familiar, poisonous vapor surrounded him, just like it had in his first encounter with the Rictus. Finn gasped as the gray ether coalesced violently all around him like an angry swarm of bees before settling on all his exposed skin.

And Finn felt it. He felt like a deer in the headlights of an oncoming eighteen-wheeler. His mind scrambled to find anything to hold onto, but he stood crippled in the face of his all-consuming horror. A million miles away, his hand clung to something, but it felt unimportant. The corners of his mouth turned up into a deathly, mirthless grin, and his mind tumbled backward into a pit of fear.

In a last-ditch effort requiring every ounce of his willpower, Finn tried to *see*. He tried to focus on what was truly real, the way he had with Kemuel months before. From the bottom of a black tunnel, Finn saw a brief flash of hope. Just a glimmer, really—a microscopic glimpse into one brief moment... But it was enough.

Finn saw Eden emerge from the forest after rescuing him. He saw the light in her eyes as she smiled at him for the first time. He saw the sun ripple in her hair, like a curtain of gold and fire and cinnamon. He saw the wonder on his own face as she approached. And he saw something in that amazed expression of his, something that reminded him of a conversation with his grandmother.

Finn focused on recreating that expression. He played and replayed the scene, desperate to reclaim that feeling. As he struggled, he saw other flashes: his mother, his grandparents, the guests of the Thin House. He pulled himself higher and higher, using each vision as leverage, until the blackness suddenly parted.

"You don't scare me!" Finn gasped, and the Rictus flinched. Finn seized his chance and raised the photo he'd taken from the attic.

"You're not a monster," he said firmly, brandishing the faded Polaroid.

"How are you still —?"

"I'm not talking to you!" Finn barked. Then, he said softly, "I'm talking to Mr. James."

Confusion flashed across the Rictus's face. Then, he laughed. "James has been silent for years, child."

"You were not always a prisoner," Finn continued.

Something slithered underneath the skin of the pale man's face, winding down his cheek and neck. The Rictus raised his arm, and the flesh parted in his palm. A thin, black tendril with a needle-sharp tip grew until it grazed Finn's neck.

Finn ignored the small trickle of blood and tried to find some sign of life in the man's face.

"You were a husband and a father!" he insisted, pressing the photograph into the pale man's line of sight.

Finn saw a flicker in the man's eyes, and the sharp tendril receded, sliding back into his palm. He reached forward slowly and took the photo, his placid gaze softening. The corners of his deathly grin drooped until his mouth became a solemn line.

A tired man stared at the small object in his hand, as if it were the first thing he'd seen in decades.

The Polaroid was old. It had taken on a slightly yellow hue. But James surely recognized the pretty young woman standing beside a younger, happier version of himself—and the little boy she held in her arms.

James squeezed his eyes shut. He raised the picture to his lips and held it there, standing motionless for some time.

Eventually, he lowered the picture and opened his eyes. He stared at Finn and nodded.

"Thank you."

Before Finn could say anything in reply, James turned around. His jaw set with steely determination, he took a step toward the well in the center of the room. When he took a second step, the black plasma receded from Ezekiel. As James got closer to the well, the last of the black mass disappeared within him. He breathed heavily, but he forced his way forward until he stumbled against the side of the well.

"Mr. James…" Finn said tentatively.

James leaned against the stone base of the well and reached for the heavy iron gate. He winced, gritting his teeth, and something lurched within him. Doubling over in pain, he clutched his stomach. His body shuddered, and something welled up under his skin along his spinal cord.

A monstrous voice roared from somewhere inside James's thin frame.

"NO!"

James groaned loudly, but he managed to fling the gate open. Realization dawned on Finn as James began to lower himself over the rim of the well. Then, James froze. His body snapped involuntarily forward then backward. He tried to steady himself against the well's base, but something expanded underneath the back of his suitcoat.

"My God..." Ezekiel whispered in horror.

The stitching tore in the back of James's suit. Finn watched in horror as something massive, black, and vaguely human-shaped burst from James's back. His body fell limply to the side, and the Rictus slowly unfurled.

Finn stared up at the monster.

In its true form, the Rictus stood over seven-feet-tall. Its skin was pitch-black and covered in a thick, oily sludge. Though the Rictus appeared humanoid, its proportions were... wrong. It had a long, thin torso and rigid, elongated arms that came to sharp points in lieu of hands. The Rictus's head was a perfect oval on a protracted neck, and the face had no eyes, ears, or nose, only a gaping mouth filled with hundreds of fine, glinting teeth and exposed, blood-red gums. It was stuck in a perpetual grin.

The creature peered at Finn through its teeth.

All the ancient symbols carved into the floor and walls began to glow blue like the crystals. As the symbols brightened, Finn heard a hissing noise like a tea kettle coming to boil. Smoke rose from the oily, black surface of the Rictus's skin. At first, Finn thought it was emiting its poison again, but he quickly realized the truth.

The room was cooking the monster alive.

The Rictus raised one of its sharp, pointed arms toward Finn. Ezekiel rushed forward in a whir of motion and caught the arm in a vice-like grip. He held tightly, glaring up into the fierce grin as he plunged his knife into the monster's chest.

The Rictus's black, oily skin hissed and bubbled as Ezekiel pushed the blade in all the way to the handle. The monster leaned down until it was inches from Ezekiel's face. A screaming hiss forced its way through the grinning teeth.

Ezekiel roared, kept one hand on the knife, and put all his weight behind a massive shove, sending the Rictus tumbling backward into the well. He stumbled and Finn stepped forward to steady him. Grandfather and grandson panted with exhaustion as they listened to the creature fall.

Mr. Gareth rejoined them, clutching Finn's sweater tightly over the wound in his chest. The Rictus hissed as it fell deeper and deeper into the darkness, and Mr. Gareth pulled the gate over the mouth of the well before sliding the heavy lock into place. The snap echoed loudly through the basement.

Finn felt something brush against him. He looked down and saw Chester, leaning wearily against his leg.

Ezekiel knelt beside James. The salesman's eyes fluttered and a pool of blood seeped from his back. Ezekiel's hand rested on his shoulder.

"Can we do anything?" he asked.

"Don't leave me down here," James whispered.

Ezekiel nodded.

"And if you can... Find my family. Make sure they're okay."

Then James's body shuddered. He sighed one last time—and was still.

Ezekiel closed the salesman's eyes, shaking his own head. "Poor man. Let's get him upstairs." Ezekiel rose to his feet.

"We should wait," Finn said, helping Mr. Gareth to stand.

"Why?" Ezekiel asked.

"The Auditor's here. Nana Eleanor's trying to stall him outside."

"What?!?"

⌂

"Mrs. Blacklock, I assure you that I am impressed with your garden and with the successes of your greenhouse, but I must insist that I speak with both you and Mr. Blacklock immediately," the Auditor said sternly as he opened the front door.

"But you have to see the orchards," Eleanor insisted, trying to cut off his view inside the house.

The Auditor leaned past Eleanor and nodded at Ezekiel, Mr. Gareth, and Finn.

"Good afternoon, gentlemen."

Mr. Gareth rose from his seat by the fire and bowed to the Auditor. "The pleasure is ours, I'm sure. How have you been, Mr. Seven?"

"Adequate. May I inquire as to your well-being, Mr. Gareth? You seem to be moving gingerly."

Mr. Gareth straightened his fresh, blue cardigan and shrugged at the otherworldly bureaucrat. The casual gesture seemed out of place for such a refined vampire-librarian.

"Oh, I'm fine. I'm just up past my bedtime. Lost track of time with young Master Finn. In fact, if you will excuse me, I think I will get some rest."

Mr. Gareth didn't wait for an answer before leaving the living room and heading toward the stairs.

The Auditor raised an eyebrow and did a cursory scan of the room.

Besides some disheveled hair and clothes, Finn and Ezekiel looked normal. They sat on the large couch watching TV, and Chester sat in front of them, eyes glued to the old episode of *Columbo*.

There was no sign of Eden or of James's body.

The Auditor wore a mildly puzzled expression.

"I'm surprised I was able to catch you at home. It was my understanding that the Sunday service you both attend normally gets out at two. Is everything in order here?" he asked.

"Oh, yes." Eleanor stepped forward and placed a hand on Ezekiel's shoulder. "With it being Lahela and

Eden's last Sunday here, I'm planning a special dinner. Came home early to start on the cooking."

"You should come by later. I'm sure we'll have biscuits and honey," Ezekiel said cheerfully.

"Perhaps," the Auditor said, staring directly at Finn. He paused for a moment, adjusted his glasses, and reached inside his suitcoat. "I have the results of your recent inspection. I think you will be pleased."

Ezekiel furrowed his brow as he took the stack of papers from the Auditor. He leafed through them and nodded, but the puzzled expression remained. "Thanks... I didn't think you dropped these off in person?"

"It is not often that property managers have such positive results. As a courtesy, I decided to deliver my approval in person."

"That is so nice of you," Eleanor said, stepping forward to take the papers from Ezekiel. She glanced at the forms then smiled at the Auditor. "I hope you'll consider coming tonight?"

"We'd love to have you," Ezekiel agreed.

And Finn knew they meant it, though he could not understand how. In spite of the major battle moments earlier, the passed-out werewolf, the dead body upstairs, and the fact that absolutely no food was anywhere near ready, Ezekiel and Eleanor wanted the Auditor to join them for dinner. They would happily prepare an incredible meal and play host to the Auditor, the one being who could take everything away, because they were Ezekiel and Eleanor Blacklock—and they invited people to dinner.

The Auditor stared at Finn again.

"I will consider attending." He nodded almost imperceptibly. "For the time being, I have other appointments. Perhaps your grandson could escort me to my vehicle?"

Ezekiel and Eleanor stared at Finn.

"Uh… Sure," Finn managed to whisper. His heart thumped hard in his chest—he knew the jig was up.

Ezekiel looked nervous as he held open the door for Finn and the Auditor. Eleanor nodded subtly in support as they passed. Chester watched anxiously as the door closed behind them.

"You've had quite the afternoon, Mr. Anglin." There was no trace of a question in the Auditor's stern, steady voice.

"Well, Eden and I mostly watched TV, but…" Finn trailed off.

The Auditor stopped walking and stared down at him.

"Mr. Anglin, I assure you I'm quite aware of the events that have taken place this afternoon. I know the Entity escaped. I know it was safely defeated. And I know it has been separated from Mr. James Farsons."

Finn felt like the ground disappeared beneath his feet. He thought of how he, Mr. Gareth, and Ezekiel had rushed upstairs and placed James's body in an empty room. He thought of Ezekiel moving Eden out of the living room, of everyone replacing their battle-damaged clothes and moving their weapons out of sight. It had all been for nothing. The Auditor was going to close the Thin House, and his grandparents would…

"Please don't fire my grandparents! It wasn't their fault, I—"

The Auditor held up a hand to stop Finn. "Mr. Anglin, why would I fire your grandparents?"

"In the report, it said—"

"You mean the report you took from my briefcase and read without my permission?"

"Yes… Sorry. But my grandparents said the Rictus escaped before, and in the report, it said they only get one warning before their contract is terminated."

"I see. Well that has a rather simple explanation," said the Auditor.

"What's that?"

"I lied."

Finn stared at the Auditor as if seeing him for the first time, noting the slightest upturn at the corners of the gentleman's mouth.

"So you're not going to fire my grandparents?" he asked nervously.

"Do you realize what has happened today, Mr. Anglin? I admit, the first time your grandparents encountered the Entity, I did not realize the significance."

"Significance of what?"

"Of how the Entity was defeated. Do you remember reading about their experience in the report?"

Finn nodded. "The report made it sound like you didn't know how they fought the Rictus. You said it was unusual for humans to be able to fight it at all."

"The Rictus and its kind are manifestations of different aspects of fear. This Entity in particular is composed of the fear that paralyzes, that makes action impossible. I believe you experienced this."

"Yeah." Finn remembered the poisonous vapor the creature emitted and the terror that seemed to consume his thoughts and freeze his body. He shuddered at the memory, and then he realized something. "But wait, I got out of that. I thought of..." Finn trailed off and blushed slightly.

"What did you think of?" the Auditor asked.

"Something my grandmother said. 'Love always wins out over fear.' I thought of people I loved, and eventually, I came out of it."

"Yes," the Auditor nodded. "Creatures like Mr. Gareth and Eden have a greater tolerance, but most humans are quickly overcome by the Entity's mental assault. Your grandparents' love allows them to see through those attacks enough to defend themselves. Your own love allowed you to overcome the paralysis enough to brandish the photo. But that is only part of what I am suggesting. Once the Rictus attaches to a human host, it is shielded from our defensive measures."

"That's why the room seemed to hurt it, when it left James."

"Yes. And I suspect it only left because James was about to imprison them both. This closely mirrors your grandparents' first encounter."

"How do you mean?"

"In my report, I detail the Entity's possession of Maximillian Fonchet. However, I was not entirely honest about the nature of your grandparents' battle with the monster. You see, when Eleanor left to help Ezekiel, she was followed. The surviving daughter of Maximilian, young Madeline, followed your grand-mother back to the scene of the massacre. She did so unbeknownst to your grandmother, and it wasn't until Ezekiel started to tire that she revealed herself.

"Madeline's presence gave Maximillian the strength to take control of the Rictus momentarily, at which point he ended his life. He sacrificed himself to keep from being used for further destruction. Without a host, the Rictus was stunned and vulnerable to Ezekiel's knife. Only then were your grandparents able to force the monster back into its prison."

"So love did beat it. Not just my grandparents', but James's and Maximillian's," Finn proposed.

"Yes. It would appear that fear's hold on man is ultimately finite. Inspiring, wouldn't you agree?"

"Yes," Finn nodded. "But why lie about Madeline in your report?"

"I thought she had been through enough. If I'd reported on her second encounter, not to mention her witnessing of me, I suspect I would have been instructed to make her stay with your grandparents at the new entry point. Instead, she was able to live a quiet, happy life, far away from where her family died."

Finn thought about the alterations to the story he and Eden had stumbled upon. He thought about the horror the Rictus wrought on so many lives, and how his grandparents built something small and wonderful in the midst of so much terror. He looked up at the neat man in the suit. From the short distance, he could see the small, silver tie pin shaped like a wing.

"Why are you letting my grandparents off the hook? I mean, I'm glad you are, but you seem to take your rules very seriously. Why even tell me this?" Finn asked.

They arrived at the car. The Auditor opened the door and set his briefcase in the passenger seat. He paused, stood by the open door, and seemed to think about Finn's questions. He reached toward his tie and loosened the Windsor knot ever so slightly. Then, he looked Finn in the eye, and Finn got the impression of something ancient behind his gaze.

"Ezekiel and Eleanor Blacklock are people of faith. In spite of all the horrors they have encountered, they hold to that faith. They believe. Not just in a benevolent higher power, but in right and wrong. That everything truly good is eternal. Their efforts to live in harmony with that faith have impacted many. They help their fellow men. They remind those whom the world calls 'monsters,' that there is good within all of us. Your grandparents treat people with respect and dignity."

Finn nodded, and the Auditor turned and looked up at the Thin House.

"Do you know what I believe in, Mr. Anglin? I believe in people like your grandparents." He looked back at Finn, and the sunlight gleamed off his glasses. "And I think well-placed faith should be rewarded, don't you?"

The Auditor turned and stepped into his car. He shut the door, but the automatic window rolled down, and he leaned out toward Finn. Finn may have imagined it, but he thought the otherworldly bureaucrat was smiling.

"You have had an interesting summer, Mr. Anglin. I expect, if you hold onto what you've learned, your life will be one of Mr. Gareth's favorite tales one day."

He started to roll up the window but paused.

"Oh. And please tell Ms. Anderson that she owes me one packet of marshmallows."

Finn said goodbye and turned to walk back up the driveway. He heard the car crank over his shoulder. When he glanced backward, he wasn't surprised to see no sign of the Auditor's vehicle.

With a shake of his head, he walked back to his grandparents' house.

⌂

Eden was awake and waiting with Ezekiel and Eleanor when Finn returned to the living room. Everyone immediately began asking questions, probing for details about his conversation with the Auditor.

"It's okay. He just wanted to ask about my summer. Oh, and Eden, he says you owe him marshmallows."

"Dang it."

Once it was clear the threat had passed, Eleanor made Eden lie down again and brought her some soup. Ezekiel took James's body outside, wrapped it neatly, and drove it into town. He muttered something to Finn about a coroner in Opossum Trot owing him a favor. Finn didn't ask any questions.

Once Eden ate her soup and started to doze, Finn volunteered to help Eleanor in the kitchen.

"So what did the Auditor *really* say?" she pressed as soon as they were alone.

"How did you know?" Finn asked.

"The Auditor doesn't make small talk. If it was just the marshmallows, I'm sure he would have spoken to Eden about it. So what's going on?"

"He knows about what happened, but he's not going to punish y'all. He just wanted to reassure me. Turns out, he really likes y'all."

"I knew it!" Eleanor smiled.

"He told me about Madeline."

"That poor girl. We kept up with her, from a distance, of course. She was able to find happiness, eventually start a family. Live a normal life. The Auditor made the right decision."

"I think so, too.

"Finn, how did you know? Ezekiel told me about the picture, and bringing Mr. Farsons out of that thing. How did you know to try that?"

"It's like what y'all always say. Our job is to remind people they aren't monsters."

Eleanor stared at Finn for a moment, then wrapped him in a hug so fierce, it put Ezekiel to shame.

"I am so proud of you."

"I love y'all. I want to keep coming to visit," he said, hugging her back with a ferocity that was impressive in its own right.

"You are always welcome here. Always."

Eleanor and Finn hugged for a few moments longer before she sent him to get some rest.

Before he settled in for a much needed repose, Finn ascended the stairs and stepped into the library. He wasn't surprised to see Mr. Gareth sitting in his chair by the fire reading *The Count of Monte Cristo*.

He rose when he noticed Finn.

"Master Finn, you should be resting after your ordeal."

"You were impaled by a monster. Maybe you should take your own advice."

"Few things relax me as much as Mr. Dumas's swashbuckling adventures. Though, I do see your point."

"I just wanted to thank you... for saving us," Finn said.

Mr. Gareth smiled warmly and removed his glasses. He polished the lenses on his sweater while he looked down at his feet. For once, the verbose vampire seemed to be struggling to say something. Eventually, he replaced his glasses and looked at Finn.

"The sentiment is appreciated, but you are mistaken. It is I who owe you my gratitude."

"What do you mean?"

"When we first met, you asked me about my story, and the adventures I've had during my long life. Do you remember what I told you?"

"You said you haven't had many adventures."

"That's right. I've thought about our conversation a lot this summer. You see, Finn, I wasn't always the... observer I am today. Before I became a vampire, there was a time that I truly lived, and even loved." Mr. Gareth paused, then smiled sadly. "So much was taken from me, Finn. However, I see now that my zest for life wasn't taken from me. It was forfeited."

"I'm not sure I understand," Finn said.

"There is a difference between surviving and really living, Master Finn. I've let fear keep me from being truly alive for over four hundred years."

Finn nodded.

"I'm not ready to revisit the story that brought me here, but seeing you grow this summer, seeing you touch the lives of so many guests... Well, I suppose it's made me want to create some new stories of my own."

Realizing it was just going to be a day for hugging, Finn embraced the old vampire.

Mr. Gareth seemed flustered for a moment, then patted Finn slowly on the shoulder.

"You're a good young man. I'm proud of you."

"Thanks, Mr. Gareth."

Finn left Mr. Gareth to his book. He walked downstairs and through the hallway without thinking about looking at the grandfather clock. He yawned as he stepped into the living room. Eden was asleep on the sofa, and he could hear the sounds of Eleanor beginning to cook coming from the kitchen. Finn smiled and exhaled.

He eventually fell asleep in the chair beside the couch where Eden reclined. Chester nuzzled in beside him, and Finn dreamed about nothing at all.

He awoke to the pleasant aroma of Eleanor's cooking. He knew before opening his eyes that Eleanor had accomplished her goal of cooking a going-away feast for Eden and Lahela. He could imagine the wonderful spread of delicious home-cooked dishes completely covering the dining room table. He saw all the guests surrounding the feast, trading stories and jokes as they enjoyed the food. He saw Mr. Gareth telling Lahela about a mermaid in Lake Pontchartrain while he ate a bowl of dark, red chili. He saw Ezekiel arm-wrestling with a visiting cyclops in town on business, Eden cheering for his grandfather. He saw Eleanor passing the Auditor a plate of biscuits, shooing Chester away from a bowl of dark chocolate pudding.

Finn imagined his grandparents dancing in the kitchen after all the guests had gone to bed. He saw himself telling Eden goodbye as she left with her mother to start over in a new place. He noticed his pained expression as he hugged her goodbye. He saw the last couple of days fly by, until it was time for his mother to pick him up. Finally, Finn saw himself stepping across the bridge—and forgetting the best summer of his life.

Without opening his eyes, Finn saw how the rest of his summer would unfold. He knew that once he opened his eyes, his course was more or less set. His magical time at his grandparents' boarding home would end. He would return home and be left with fragments of memory and whatever lessons he could pull from the experience. Finn knew, at one point, that would have frightened him.

It did not frighten him anymore.

Finn opened his eyes.

EPILOGUE

Finn couldn't focus on his teacher's lecture. She was discussing Greek mythology, a subject that normally interested him, but her words couldn't hold his attention.

He was having another headache. Ever since his mother picked him up from his grandparents' house, headaches sprang up at odd times. They weren't painful—they were barely headaches at all, more like sudden waves of confusion—as if his mind were climbing a set of stairs and suddenly missed a step.

Finn tried to figure out a common cause, but they seemed to come on at random: when he went to the library, when a rabbit crossed his path at the park, and a particularly strong one when he'd taken a box to the attic for his mom. As he pondered the headaches, he remembered the peculiar conversation with his mom on the drive home from his grandparents' house.

He'd been very excited to tell her all about his grandparents, but he couldn't remember many specifics about his visit. He knew he'd had a wonderful time—he just couldn't say why. He'd spoken with his grandmother on the phone the night he'd gotten home, but she seemed to steer the conversation away from specifics of the summer.

Despite not remembering much about his summer, Finn found that he'd returned home... thinking things, knowing things. Odd things. He watched an action movie with his mom, and he knew the hero was holding his gun wrong. He'd been able to demonstrate the correct grip using a banana from the kitchen. He corrected his teacher on a detail about the Duke of Wellington, but he had no idea how he knew the fact in question. Finn even discovered that he now found big grins off-putting and marshmallows hilarious.

Sighing, he tried to make himself pay attention to his teacher's lecture on Achilles and Hector, but then something else kept him from focusing.

He felt eyes lingering on the back of his head.

For the life of him, Finn couldn't figure out why the new girl seemed so interested in him. He hadn't heard her name when the teacher introduced her—he'd been too busy staring. But she promptly noticed him and smiled.

Her smile caused a flutter in his chest, followed by one of the strange headaches. Ever since, he'd felt the pretty girl with the auburn hair and athletic build staring at him from two seats behind. When he turned his head slightly, he could see her watching him out the corner of his eye.

Finn didn't know where he got the confidence, but he turned in his seat. He looked directly at the new girl, and he smiled.

She beamed at him for a moment and then winked. When she did, her eyes flashed and took on a yellow hue.

Finn couldn't say why the new girl's eyes were so familiar—but he was excited to find out.

Acknowledgements

This book represents the efforts of many patient, long-suffering indiviuals. I would like to thank my editor Julie Elise Landry for her hard work and encouragement as a rough collection of stories was shaped into something much more polished and professional. I would also like to thank Teo Skaffa for the cover art and my grandmother Judy Nickens for the art on the dedication page. Finally, a special thank you to the rest of my family and friends, who tolerated my constant chatter about this story—especially my wife, who listened patiently to hundreds of versions of the story that eventually became *The Thin House*.

About the Author

Jake Nickens was born and raised in southern Mississippi. He spent his childhood listening to family tall tales and reading comic books that turned him into the kind of adult who writes stories about jackalopes and vampire-librarians. He enjoys watching old boxing matches, reading mystery novels, and trying to make an edible gluten-free biscuit. He lives in Mississippi with his wife Lydia, their pitbull Evie, and their cat Muffin.

Made in the USA
Coppell, TX
02 May 2020